A Heart
for All Time

by

Linda Tillis

A Heart for All Time

Cover Art by *Debbie Taylor*

The Wild Rose Press, Inc.
PO Box 708
Adams Basin, NY 14410-0708
Visit us at www.thewildrosepress.com

Publishing History
First American Rose Edition, 2018
Print ISBN 978-1-5092-1964-3
Digital ISBN 978-1-5092-1965-0

Published in the United States of America

Thank you, Jesus. **She ran to the man. They had** obviously not bothered tying his hands, because he was desperately holding on to the rope above his head. He was not dead, but she didn't know how long that fact would hold if she couldn't get him down. She took a split second to look after the fleeing horsemen and watched as they rounded a wall of rock and disappeared from view. She immediately grabbed the man's feet and placed them on her shoulders.

"Stand still," she shouted up at him. "Don't panic! I've got you."

Once he got still, Sarah's height put enough slack on the rope for him to loosen the noose and jerk it over his head. And none too soon, as they both collapsed to the ground a few seconds later. Sarah had dropped her pistol when she grabbed the man's feet. She picked it up now, dusted it off on her jacket, and returned it to her leg holster.

The man called Kramer was coughing, trying to drag in enough breath to make up for what had seemed like an eternity that he was without air. He was lying on his side, eyes closed, coughing and thanking the Lord, when he felt hands on his head. His survival instincts kicked in, and he lashed out with a fist that made solid contact.

"Hey! It's okay, mister. I'm just trying to make sure you're all right."

Aaron opened his eyes, and they confirmed what his mind had told him but he had refused to believe. It was a woman who had saved him. A woman holding a hand over one eye and scrambling away from him on her backside.

Also by Linda Tillis
and available from The Wild Rose Press, Inc.

A MAN WITH A PURE HEART
In rural Florida, 1910, a police detective and a schoolteacher seek her sister's murderer, hoping to bring him to justice. When the killer finds them instead, events take a darker turn, and the detective must race against time to save the woman he has fallen in love with.

Dedication

This book is dedicated to the backbone of every law enforcement agency: the highly trained, detail-oriented, steady-as-a-rock dispatcher; that woman or man who is truly the first responder; the one who hears the screams of hysteria and still manages to extract the information a responding officer or deputy needs to stay alive; the one who consoles and soothes, and instructs the mother whose child is not breathing, or the little old wife who cannot perform CPR on her husband. Then, when the responding officer arrives, the dispatcher disconnects, takes a deep breath, and answers the next ringing emergency line. Again, and again.

~*~

And to my Beau, who held me when I cried,
after my twelve-hour shifts
of trying to help save lives over the phone.
Again, and again.

Acknowledgments

A big thank you to Susan Kemp and Cindy Stafford Pontbriand for being great Beta Readers, and even greater friends.

Preface

The fire had burned low, leaving only the glowing embers to light the faces of those gathered at the feet of the tribe historian. He had promised to tell the story of the spirit woman who travelled across the sky and through time.

She was called Ai'yana, the eternal blossom, and like the exploding star that flies across the sky, she had a streak of white in her coal-black hair. Her eyes were dark blue, like the sky on a late summer evening.

She was a Thunderer, who controlled the thunder and lightning. And when she streaked across the great skies, she rode on the back of a huge a-ha-wi.

The beautiful Ai'yana had travelled through time from the beginning, always searching for a mortal man to father her a son. After a few years, she would move on, through time, searching for another deserving mortal. But she always sent a woman to care for the child left behind, a woman with a heart for all time.

Linda Tillis

Chapter One

Greeneville, Tennessee, August 2016

Sarah Haskins looked at the clock on her computer as she connected with the next ringing line. *Lord, please let my replacement be on time. If I have one more death call this day, it will send me right over the edge.*

"9-1-1, what's the address of your emergency?"

"Hello, is this the fire department?"

"We dispatch for fire, ma'am. What is the address of your emergency?" Sarah said firmly.

"Well…I don't know if it's an emergency…" The voice faded away. If a voice could paint a picture, then Sarah was talking to a frail little woman with white hair.

"Ma'am, what is your address?" *Why couldn't they just answer the questions? It would make her life so much easier.*

"Dear, could you send a fire truck with a tall ladder out here? My little Whiskers is stuck up in a tree and won't come down, and I'm afraid she is going to starve…" Now the fading voice was accompanied by tears.

"Ma'am, I cannot send you a fire truck to get your Whiskers down. Do you have a can of tuna in the house?"

"Well, yes, I think so," answered the "white-haired" voice.

"All right, sweetie, I want you to open the tuna can all the way and take the top completely off the can. Now, take it outside and wave it around under the tree so Whiskers can see you. Then set the can down at the base of the tree and go back inside. I promise you, Whiskers will come down to eat. Okay?"

Thank the Lord! There was Beverly coming through the door now.

"Did you hear me, dear?"

"Yes…are you sure she will come down?" came the tearful inquiry.

"If she's not down by tomorrow morning, then you just call us right back, okay?" Sarah used her most soothing voice as she gathered her things together. And tomorrow it would be someone else's problem, because Sarah had the next three weeks off. She hadn't taken a vacation in years and had accrued the limit in comp time. So it was vacation time, whether she liked it or not.

"All right, young lady, and thank you."

"So, how did the good folks of Greene County treat you today?" Beverly asked, as she sat in the still warm chair and adjusted her headset.

"Honey, I am so glad to see you I could just kiss you. I've had two heart attacks, both DOA, one suspicious package that shut the high school down for two hours, and a possible meth lab explosion out toward Parrotsville, off the 340, that had traffic backed up most of the morning. Let's just say there's a glass of wine screaming my name, and I'm about to go shut it up."

Beverly laughed as she plugged herself into the computer. "Well, go ahead and have a glass for me, 'cause you know my night's not gonna be a bit better. Try to enjoy your vacation."

"Oh, don't you worry about that. I've got three long weeks to purge this place from my head."

Sarah stuffed her jump-bag behind the seat of her truck and headed for home. Home to an empty cabin that was too big for her, on twenty-three acres that kept her separated from any neighbors. She could feel the adrenalin levels start to taper off as she drove. When you had no personal life, and your co-workers were the closest thing to family that you could claim, your job became all-consuming.

It had been all right when Uncle Fred was still alive. Caring for him helped her forget the really bad choices she had made.

She could barely remember the faces of her parents. She'd been seven years old when they skidded off the mountain near Gatlinburg. Fred and Thelma had taken her in and loved her as if she'd been theirs all along. They were much older than her parents, so her upbringing was a little different than most of her school friends. While other kids played video games and attended dances and such, Sarah learned to hunt and fish. She knew how to sew her own clothes, and she was a pretty darn good cook, which was handy after Aunt Thelma was diagnosed with cancer. So instead of going off to college, Sarah had taken a local job, with the Greene County Sheriff's Office, to better care for the only family she had left.

It was completely dark when she turned off the main road, checked her mailbox, and started her favorite part of the drive home. If she was lucky, she might see some deer. Those beautiful, sweet faces always seemed to calm her. It kept her from "seeing" the faces of the voices she dealt with during the day: the little old lady screaming that her husband was having a heart attack, so hysterical that you couldn't get her to even try CPR; or the single mom screaming in the background as her boyfriend beat her senseless for the third time this year.

Sarah exhaled slowly and deeply, trying to banish all the ugliness from her mind, as she parked the truck behind the cabin.

The motion detectors lit up the exterior of what could only be called a rustic palace. Her uncle had covered the two acres nearest the cabin with gardens to rival anything seen on television. Aunt Thelma's happiness was all that had mattered to him, and in the weeks before her passing, he'd wheel her into the gardens to spend hours reading to her.

That was true love. That was the kind of love Sarah had witnessed growing up, and she would never settle for less again. She was depending on the good Lord to lead her to the right man, next time around. If there ever was a next time.

At twenty-four, Sarah had married a deputy. Carl had been handsome, a little edgy, and new in town. After a whirlwind courtship, they'd settled into what she'd believed would be her dream come true. Wrong. A year into the marriage, Carl put in for a transfer to B-squad, which put them working on opposite days and nights. He claimed it was so he could be closer to the in-town action and make himself more eligible for promotion. As it turned out, the only thing Carl was promoting was a good time. Sarah found herself the object of pity when a seventeen-year-old high-school senior announced that Carl was the father of her soon-to-be-born baby.

Devoting herself to caring for her uncle had kept Sarah sane during the whole debacle of Carl's firing, the divorce, and his subsequent jail sentence. Three years later found her coming home to an empty house and an equally empty life.

There were few things nowadays that gave her joy, but tomorrow she was going to relish one of those few. She had three weeks to go hunting for antiques.

****

Asheville had some of the finest antique stores in the South, and Sarah was looking for something unique but affordable.

"Oh, shoot," she said aloud, as she pulled the truck over to check her GPS. She must have written the address down wrong. She had searched the internet for a new place to "hunt." She looked all around but could not find Anna's Gifts & Notions anywhere. She was about to give up and go find some food when she spotted a small sign down an alley. She eased the truck down the narrow, brick-lined lane, and there it was.

She was looking at a small brick building with green shutters. From the outside, it might have been any small, faded family business. But once Sarah stepped inside, she felt a shiver run across her shoulders. She knew she was going to find an exciting treasure here. The building was deceptively small from the outside; once she was inside, it seemed to go on forever. There were cases filled with glassware and old jewelry pieces. She could see the owner had set up little vignettes here and there: a beautiful chair accompanied by a Louis XIV side table, a wingback chair with a matching, brocade footstool.

Sarah must have wandered around for at least twenty minutes before a melodious voice startled her.

"Were you searching for something in particular, dear?"

She turned to find a slender woman standing behind her. Sarah was speechless at her appearance: the woman's head was covered in shiny, jet black hair, except for an inch-wide streak of pure white that ran from the left temple back to a lovely chignon; her prominent cheekbones and Romanesque nose spoke of Native American heritage, but her eyes were a deep, dark blue. They reminded Sarah of a stormy sky.

She smiled at Sarah and tried again. "Are you interested in furniture, jewelry, or maybe pottery?"

Sarah reddened, as she realized she had been staring at the woman.

"I'm sorry. I didn't mean to stare, but you remind me of a beautiful old painting that belonged to my uncle."

The woman stood silently. After another embarrassing pause, she turned and started down an aisle.

"Come along, dear. I pride myself on helping people find just what their hearts desire."

As Sarah followed her, it suddenly came to her why the woman looked so familiar. It wasn't just the hair; the woman wore a suede dress that hung loosely against her slim body. The neckline was covered in beautiful bead embroidery. Sarah shook her head. She would have to look more closely at the painting in the den, but she would be willing to swear this woman could have stepped right out of it. How odd.

The woman stepped behind a glass case and observed Sarah, as if interested in her reaction.

Sarah looked down into the case and drew in a slow breath. She could feel her heart pick up its rhythm. She was seeing some of the most breathtaking pieces of beaded jewelry she had ever come across in all her shopping trips. There were bracelets, brooches, and necklaces of all shapes and sizes. One piece held her frozen to the spot. It was an upper arm bangle. The shape, a winding snake, was common in a piece of this type, and it was the jeweled look of the beads that called to Sarah. They were arranged in such a pattern as to perfectly resemble a copperhead snake, with its head drawn back as if ready to strike. The eyes were a golden-colored glass that seemed to speak to Sarah. She was so engrossed in study of the piece that she was startled when the woman spoke.

"She is lovely, isn't she?"

Sarah stuttered, "Excuse me?"

"The goddess. She is lovely."

"The goddess? Do you mean the snake?" Sarah raised her eyes to the woman. The woman was smiling indulgently, as if Sarah were a child drooling over a piece of candy.

"Would you like to try it on?"

Sarah looked on eagerly as the woman opened the case and removed the bangle.

Sarah was not a thin girl. She carried twenty pounds more than her doctor was happy about. Years of working in the garden, carrying a rifle in the woods, and pushing first Aunt Thelma and then Uncle Fred in a wheelchair had developed some muscle in her upper arms, besides. There was a moment of insecurity as the woman extended the armlet. She would be embarrassed if it was too small.

It happened so quickly that Sarah was not sure what she'd seen. It was almost as if the jewelry had come alive and wrapped itself around her upper arm.

"It fits you perfectly."

Sarah glanced at the woman and thought she saw traces of a smug smile. As if this exotic woman knew something she did not. No, she must have imagined it.

"Yes," she sighed, "it does fit nicely. And it's beautiful. But where in the world would I wear it?"

Sarah looked back into the case. There was a piece that was more her style. A beautiful, arrowhead-shaped piece of Tennessee Paint Rock Agate. It was suspended from a rope of aged rawhide.

"How about that arrowhead necklace? I would get much more use out of that."

She reached down to remove the bangle from her arm. When she tugged on it, there was a quick sting. She looked down at her arm. The bangle had come off easily, and lay coiled in the palm of her hand, but something on it must have caught on her arm, because she found two little drops of blood where the bangle had been.

"Oh, dear," the woman exclaimed. "I am so sorry. You must have scratched yourself." She immediately produced a tissue and wiped away the droplets.

Sarah could barely see where they'd been. She handed the bangle back to the woman. "Could I see the arrowhead?"

"Of course." The woman placed the beautiful

bangle back in the case carefully and then handed the rawhide rope to Sarah.

She held the smooth, cool, agate piece in the palm of her hand as she asked, "How much for this one?"

The woman smiled sweetly. "Well, this lone piece used to be part of a pair. They were said to be magical, when worn by lovers. Since I have only the one to offer you, why don't I just give it to you, as an apology for the scratch?"

Sarah considered those dark blue eyes. "Are you sure?"

"Oh, yes, I am sure. Your heart knows this piece was made for you."

The woman's assertive tone made Sarah a little uncomfortable.

"All right, and thank you."

The woman started moving toward the front door. "Was there something else I can help you with?"

Sarah thought she was being brushed off, but she didn't mind, as she was suddenly tired. *Must be all the overtime I've put in lately.*

She followed the woman to the door. "No, ma'am, I think this will do me."

The woman smiled as she held open the door. "Yes, the heart knows what it wants."

Sarah heard the click of the lock behind her as she headed for her truck.

****

Sarah looked at the clock. Five-thirty. She had taken a shower, thinking it would freshen her up, maybe wash away this tiredness. She was dressed in her newest jeans, matching jacket, and her favorite boots, with her revolver strapped above the boot top. The whole ensemble paired very well with her new arrowhead necklace. But now she wasn't sure she had enough energy to ride all the way into Greeneville for supper.

"Heck," she said to the empty kitchen, "I'm not even hungry now."

She opened the fridge, took out a full bottle of Sangria, and was reaching for a glass when she remembered the painting.

"Aha! That's what I was going to do."

Sarah moved to the back of the cabin, taking along the bottle and glass.

Both Thelma and Fred had been avid readers. He, of course, lived for the hunting magazines that arrived regularly, while Thelma had been a "closet" romance reader. Uncle Fred had built a fireplace in the back wall of the cabin, and Aunt Thelma had arranged two reclining chairs in front of the beautiful river-rock wall, with an antique table between them to hold their bowls of ice cream. This had been their favorite retreat, the place where they spent hours reading and dozing, completely comfortable in their love.

Sarah set her bottle and glass on the table, then turned to the inner wall. Yep, there it was. Uncle Fred had once told her the painting had been in the family for several generations. She moved closer now, to better see the details.

"By golly," she exclaimed. "I was right!"

There, before her eyes, was the woman from the store. Same streak of white in her hair, standing in a forest, with beams of golden light shining around her. There was a large stag with his head thrown back, as if challenging her presence in his domain. She had one hand extended toward him, as if to calm him. When Sarah was a little girl she would pretend the woman was an Indian princess and the stag was going to turn into a handsome warrior and claim his love.

"Good heavens," Sarah yelped aloud. There, on the woman's extended arm, was the snake bangle! Well, *a* snake bangle. Surely not the one from the store.

She moved to one of the recliners and turned it to face the painting. She opened the bottle and poured a full glass of the cold, sweet wine. She got comfortable in the recliner and just stared at the painting. She sipped occasionally, as she tried to make sense of it all.

Chapter Two

Viking Mountain, Tennessee, August 1890

Sarah was dreaming. Men were arguing. She was cold. She must have kicked the blanket off the bed. She reached out for the blanket, and felt...dirt? The men were louder now. She must have left the television on. *All right, all right, I'll just have to get up and turn it off.*

Sarah opened her eyes and found herself looking at treetops...and blue sky! She rolled to her side and could see she was lying on the ground...cold, hard ground. And the arguing men were blocked from her view by a thick stand of mountain laurel. Some were laughing, and one was yelling.

Sarah froze. What the heck was going on? She slowly removed the revolver from her ankle holster. One voice stood out above the others, and what he said made her blood run cold.

"Taggart, you'll never get away with killing me. You'll be the prime suspect when I come up missing."

"Hell, Kramer, they'll think you finally fell off the deep end and hung yourself. That's if they ever find your body. I mean, we are a far piece up the mountain, and why would they come lookin' up here?"

"Folks'll just say the poor soul couldn't get over his wife disappearin' while he was off roundin' up horses. Add to that how he was stuck with that kid who never spoke. Got the best of him, livin' in that house...lookin' at all those pictures he drew."

There was the laughter again.

"And after a few months, I'll just ride into Greeneville and lay a claim on the place, pay any back taxes, and it'll all be mine."

Sarah crawled closer to the bushes. She could just make out a man on a horse. His back was to her, but she could clearly see the rope around his neck. Oh, Lord! She had no idea how many men there were. Her gun only held five rounds. Without even realizing it, she started to pray. "Please, Lord, help me. Please don't let them hang this man, Lord."

Before she could think of more to ask for, there was a slapping sound, a horse screamed, and hooves thundered as the animal fled. Then all was quiet.

After what seemed like a lifetime, she heard other horses leaving. She edged her way around the bushes, and there he was. Dangling.

Thank you, Jesus. She ran to the man. They had obviously not bothered tying his hands, because he was desperately holding on to the rope above his head. He was not dead, but she didn't know how long that fact would hold if she couldn't get him down. She took a split second to look after the fleeing horsemen and watched as they rounded a wall of rock and disappeared from view. She immediately grabbed the man's feet and placed them on her shoulders.

"Stand still," she shouted up at him. "Don't panic! I've got you."

Once he got still, Sarah's height put enough slack on the rope for him to loosen the noose and jerk it over his head. And none too soon, as they both collapsed to the ground a few seconds later. Sarah had dropped her pistol when she grabbed the man's feet. She picked it up now, dusted it off on her jacket, and returned it to her leg holster.

The man called Kramer was coughing, trying to drag in enough breath to make up for what had seemed like an eternity that he was without air. He was lying on his side, eyes closed, coughing and thanking the Lord, when he felt hands on his head. His survival instincts kicked in, and he lashed out with a fist that made solid contact.

"Hey! It's okay, mister. I'm just trying to make sure you're all right."

Aaron opened his eyes, and they confirmed what his mind had told him but he had refused to believe. It was a woman who had saved him. A woman holding a hand over one eye and scrambling away from him on her backside.

"Whoo…" He tried to speak, only to find his voice was so weak and raspy even he could barely hear it.

"Don't try to talk. You may have damage to your larynx. You're going to need to see an ENT to determine how much damage has been done."

The woman removed her hand from her face. Aaron could see she was going to have a real shiner soon. Lord, he had done that to her.

He tried again. "Ma'am…" Again there was only a weak croaking sound.

"Look, mister, I know what I'm talking about. Stop trying to talk. Now, where is your truck parked? Your horse is probably waiting for you at the trailer."

The man had a look of total confusion on his face. He started to stand but began to sway a little. He leaned against the tree to keep from falling.

The woman spoke again.

"Just bend over and let some blood get to your head. It's the shock. You're probably going to…" and before she could finish, the man vomited violently. He staggered back against the tree and slid down to the ground again.

He just sat there looking up at Sarah. He was content to wait for his strength to return. The resignation was evident, in his eyes.

Good. Now, how to get him home?

Most of Sarah's life had been spent taking care of others. She had received awards from the 911 Center for her quick actions and her calm handling of life-threatening situations. Shootings, premature births, bank robberies—they were all old hat to Sarah.

But saving a man from hanging, *from murder*, had occupied her mind for the last several minutes. Now she looked around her, and confusion washed over her. *Where the heck am I, and how in the world did I get here?*

"Kramer."

The man looked up at her in surprise.

"One of those men called you that."

He nodded.

"Look, mister, I know I told you not to talk, but I'm a little confused. Where are we, and how did I get here?"

****

Aaron Kramer finally took a good look at the woman who had saved his life. She was tall, for a woman, made more so by those fancy boots she was sportin'. Her hair was dark, not quite black but near

17

enough, and was pulled back and tied with a bandana. That she was built to have kids was plain to see. No woman should be wearing pants that tight—or at all, for that matter.

Aaron pointed to her and gave the universal signal of a shoulder shrug and widespread hands. He had no idea who she was.

"Yes." She nodded, trying to keep calm. "We don't know each other. I understand that. But I fell asleep in my recliner, in my home off Snapps Ferry Road, and I woke up here. Where the hell is here?"

Aaron tried to answer but could only manage a hoarse, painful-sounding whisper.

"All right. This is not doing either of us any good. Look, if you can manage to walk, just take me to your vehicle, and we'll go from there."

Aaron held onto the tree as he rose to his full six feet and four inches. He waited, expecting the weakness to return. When he was sure it had passed, he started walking quickly. He had to get home and make sure Jeremy was okay. The poor kid had seen enough tragedy. Aaron had to let him know he was alive.

****

Sarah picked up her pace to keep up with his long strides, but she barely noticed his seeming need to hurry, or her surroundings, as her mind was running wild, trying to figure out what the heck was going on. It seemed as if she must still be asleep, but the cool, mountain air told her otherwise. As they rounded the rock wall, where the would-be murderers had disappeared, she was overcome by a sense of déjà vu.

"Kramer, wait a minute."

He turned back toward Sarah and waited.

She looked all around her. That formation of rocks to her right looked familiar; something about the way they seemed to hang over the side of the mountain spoke to her. She walked closer and peered out across the valley far below.

She turned back to the man. "Is this Viking Mountain? I've been here before, but where is the road? What happened to the parking lot? It looks familiar, but different."

She realized that was too many questions in a row.

"I'm sorry. Is this Viking Mountain?"

Aaron nodded yes.

"Okay, what happened to the parking lot?"

He moved his head slowly, side to side.

Sarah was nearing the end of her patience. She was trying desperately to fight off the fear that something was badly wrong.

"Never mind," she snapped. "Just keep walking."

After an hour of following a horse trail, in a steady decline, she could see out across the valley from a more level perspective. The bad feeling was getting worse. They had passed none of the bike trails or photo-op areas, and she could see no rooftops spreading across the valley floor.

They should have come upon Jones Meadow by now, where she had fully expected his truck to be parked. Surely he had not ridden a horse half way up the mountain.

Sarah was telling herself to keep calm when, all at once, the man wheeled and ran toward her. He grabbed her by the shoulders and literally threw her into the bushes at the side of the horse trail. All the wind was forced out of her when she hit the ground. That turned out to be a good thing. While she was trying to draw in air, she heard the horse approaching.

She rolled to her side and grabbed the pistol again.

She saw Kramer hunker down on the opposite side of the trail. The rider was almost on top of him when Kramer jumped up, waving both arms, which caused the horse to rear up. The rider lost his balance and fell. He had no sooner hit the ground when he bounded back up, pistol in hand.

"Damn, Kramer, you're a hard man to kill. Taggart ain't gonna like me puttin' holes in you, but I can't hang you again by myself."

As he raised his gun, Sarah spoke behind him.

"Mister, I wouldn't do that."

The man began a startled spin, firing as he turned. Fortunately for Sarah, he was caught off guard by her voice and fired before he had completely faced her. He missed by several inches.

Sarah did not. She hit him square in the chest as he continued to spin, and from the distance of six feet there was no way for her to miss his heart.

The look of surprise on his face would have been comical under any other circumstances, but Sarah had never killed a man before and did not find this humorous.

She stood there, stunned. It had all happened so fast. There had been no time to think, only enough to respond to the fact that it was him or her.

She was still staring at the body on the ground, when Aaron stepped over it and took the gun from Sarah's hand. He caught her before she hit the ground.

****

Aaron shook his head in wonder. This has been one

hell of a day, he thought, as he held on to the woman in front of him. He'd rolled Ryker's body over the cliff, managed to catch his horse before it got too far down the mountain, and mounted the skittish roan, with the woman over his shoulder. Once he got her situated in front of him, he'd headed for home. He was worried about Jeremy. The boy had lost his mama under suspicious circumstances, and had not spoken a word since. The Lord only knew what this day was doing to the boy.

Aaron remembered the happy, carefree child Jeremy had been three years ago. He would sing to butterflies, and to the squirrels in the trees. His childhood chattering had been punctuated with giggles. But now his life was silent. The sparkle was gone from those deep blue eyes, and a smile never crossed his face. He'd taken the terror of losing his mama and locked it away, never to be shared.

Aaron tightened his arm around the woman to prevent her slipping sideways. He didn't want her to fall off, but he had to hurry and find Jeremy before it got pitch dark. He had to get home.

Home was a three-room cabin on a hundred acres, fifty of which lay in the valley below Viking Mountain and fifty that ran up the mountainside. It was just a place to sleep now, to sleep and try not to dream. It had been a home once. Anna and Jeremy had stood in the doorway in the evenings and smiled their welcoming love for him. But the last time he had seen that beautiful sight had been two years ago. And Anna had been waving goodbye. He'd had no reason to think it would be the last time he'd see her beautiful smile. As the years slowly passed, her memory faded. He and Jeremy lived quiet lives now, each facing his own internal demons.

Aaron Kramer descended from a long line of horse people. They'd been gifted with a firm touch and a soft way of talking that seemed to take the wild right out of a horse. But Aaron had another talent. He was an artist. He could capture a person's soul on paper. It was a wonderful gift but didn't earn him enough money to support a family.

So he'd been excited and grateful when a man approached him about training three horses for the Derby. The money would be enough to build on to the cabin and buy a few niceties for Anna. An English gentleman had shipped three fine Arabians to Wilmington. Aaron would pick them up and train them for the Kentucky Derby and then let the man know when they were ready. How the hell was Aaron to know that Anna would disappear and Jeremy would become forever silent before he could get back from North Carolina?

When he lost Anna, he lost hope for the future. He returned the horses and the money the next year. He couldn't maintain the discipline needed to train a good horse. His heart had gone into hiding, and he'd devoted his life to caring for his now silent son.

He hadn't known he'd stopped living and was only existing, until today. When Taggart's men took him this morning, he knew he had so much more life to live and share with Jeremy. He'd closed his heart and mind to a future, but just as that damn fool horse took out from under him, he accepted that he'd been wasting his opportunities.

And then the Lord had sent him an angel. A tall

angel. One that had saved his sorry hide. The Lord must not be through with him yet. He must have some little thing left for him to do.

The woman began to stir as Aaron turned Ryker's horse toward the barn.

"Hold on, ma'am. We're almost home," he whispered hoarsely. Aaron shook his head at that. It was the first time in two years he'd thought of this place as home.

Sarah regained consciousness slowly. Good grief, she was having the craziest dream. Something about mountain climbing, and shooting people. Oh, and the hanging.

She became aware of strong arms holding her. It had been so long since she'd experienced the feeling of a hard chest against her back. She snuggled back up against that chest, and was rewarded by the sharp exhalation of hot breath her move elicited. Those strong arms tightened around her, and her breasts began to tingle. Sarah's mind told her it was time to wake up and participate fully in this warm, fuzzy dream.

She opened her eyes. She was gazing into an almost dark barn. Not a barn she was familiar with, and what was she doing on a horse? In an instant, she was fully awake, and scared to death. She took a deep breath, drew her bent arm quickly forward, then jabbed a lethal elbow backward into the ribs of whoever was holding her. Her captor grunted with surprise and instinctively loosened his hold. She immediately threw one leg over the horse's head and bailed off to the side. Sarah hit the ground hard and rolled away from the now dancing horse. She grabbed for her weapon, only to find an empty holster. She staggered to her feet and turned to confront her assailant.

Aaron just sat there on the now calm horse, staring at her like she was a crazy person. He was rubbing his rib cage with one hand and holding her pistol with the other.

"What are you doing with my gun? Give it here."

Aaron looked at the gun. Well, she had saved him from hanging, so the odds were good that she wasn't going to shoot him. He stared at her for several seconds before he tossed the pistol to her. Then he just ignored her and dismounted.

Sarah looked around. She had no freaking idea where she was. Men had been trying to kill this guy all day. For all she knew, he deserved it. She just wanted to go home and forget this day.

Oh, Lord, she needed to call the sheriff's office and let them know she had killed a man.

"Okay, Kramer, where is your phone? I've got to call the law and let them know what happened. I mean, I shot a man." Sarah's voice rose, and she could hear herself getting hysterical. She took several deep, calming breaths.

Aaron threw the horse's reins at the hitching post and ran toward the cabin.

Sarah had no choice but to follow; however, she did so from a distance, keeping the gun in her hand.

She took stock of the cabin in the waning light. No lights on inside. Very rough-hewn porch railings. This must be his weekend getaway.

Aaron shoved open the door and entered, while Sarah waited just outside. It was near dark in there, and she wasn't taking any chances.

She could hear the man trying to speak, even as she

heard the strike of a match and smelled the sulfur in the air. She couldn't make out what he was grunting. The inside of the cabin began to glow with a weak, yellow light.

Sarah stepped into the doorway. She looked around the room, then shook her head.

"Well, if you were going for ancient chic, you nailed it." The kitchen table and chairs were all primitive wood. There was a red-and-white gingham tablecloth with matching curtains.

Aaron grabbed the lantern and began opening doors as if she hadn't spoken. There was a room on each side of the open dining area. He seemed to be searching for something.

Sarah was finally able to decipher his mumbling. He was calling to someone named Jeremy. When this Jeremy did not show himself, the man headed back to the kitchen.

She looked on as he took a jar, a bottle, and a bowl from a shelf. He poured a small amount of liquid from the bottle. She caught the pungent odor of vinegar. Then he tipped the jar, and a thick, golden liquid oozed over the side. *Ahh...he's making something to soothe his throat.* Sarah took another look around the room and spotted a row of drawings lined up neatly on a chest of drawers. She stepped closer to examine them. There were several of a boy about six years old. The drawings had captured a spark of humor and curiosity in those eyes.

She moved to the next ones, then suddenly had to reach out and hold on to the chest. These were of a woman. A beautiful woman. A woman wearing a loose-fitting dress with what appeared to be beadwork around the neck. The woman had dark hair, except for that one streak of pure white. Sarah did not turn to face the man. She did not want him to see the fear that must be showing all over her face.

"Kramer, who are these people?" She hoped he didn't notice the quiver in her voice.

When she got no reply, she turned to see the man lighting another lantern. Before she could ask him again, he ran out the back door. She could see the lantern light moving up the mountainside. It continued for about fifty yards before suddenly disappearing. Sarah just stood there, waiting. She was alone in a strange man's cabin. She turned and surveyed the room. Surely he must have a cell phone somewhere. She moved back to the chest of drawers and opened the top one. Nothing but art supplies: charcoal pieces in a jar, a few pencils, and a stack of drawing paper. No cell phone. She closed that drawer and opened the next.

Before her mind registered the contents, a growl, coming from the back doorway, startled her so badly she squealed and slammed the drawer on her fingers.

She turned to see Aaron and a young boy staring at her. Aaron's face was furious. The boy's face was wet with tears but completely void of expression. It was as if all his feelings were locked so deep inside that the muscles of his face were no longer needed. Then it hit her—this was the child in the drawings. As least she thought he was. This boy's face held no curiosity…or any other emotion, for that matter.

Sarah could feel her face redden; she was embarrassed at having been caught snooping. She rubbed her still stinging fingers as she snapped at him.

"I'm not stealing anything. I was just looking for

your cell phone. Surely you didn't bring a child up here without having a phone for emergencies. And this is an emergency. I need to call the sheriff and let them know what happened and where to find the body."

The boy stayed motionless in the doorway as Aaron slowly moved toward her.

She turned her back to him and again looked at the drawings.

"I asked you before, who are these people?"

Sarah could feel the heat from his body as he moved close behind her.

In a hoarse whisper that filled her nostrils with a hint of vinegar, honey, and whiskey, he answered, "My son. My son and my wife."

Sarah looked again at the boy in the doorway. He was wearing long shorts gathered into a band just below the knees. The same as in the drawings. In the corner of each drawing was what appeared to be—but could not possibly be—a date. 1886. 1887.

"And where is she now?" Sarah asked softly.

"She died two years ago."

"And what year was that?" she asked as she turned to face him.

He looked down at her for several long moments before answering, "Eighteen eighty-eight."

Sarah lowered her eyes to prevent him from seeing her panic. It did not help when they settled on his crotch and there were buttons on the fly. No zipper. Buttons.

Sarah grabbed handfuls of his shirt.

"What year is this?" she yelled. She could hear herself yelling, but she couldn't help it.

****

Aaron gazed down at her. There were beads of

27

sweat on her upper lip. Her eyes were wide and reminded him of a trapped rabbit. At that moment, he wanted to draw her. He wanted to capture the fear and insecurity he saw in those eyes. He sensed these were not common emotions for this woman.

He placed his hands over hers, as they threatened to rip his shirt apart, and whispered hoarsely, "This is the year of our Lord eighteen ninety, the month of August."

****

Sarah had been watching his face carefully as he answered, looking for any sign of deceit or mockery. All she found was concern, and maybe pity. She turned to the boy, but his eyes held nothing.

She paced the central room of the cabin, ranting and wailing, for at least half an hour. It was a testament to the man's calm nature that he quietly prepared food for the boy as he watched her. Well, that and the fact that he could barely speak. Not that anything he might have said would have helped.

She finally dropped into a chair, laid her head down on the table, and wept herself to sleep.

Chapter Three

The smell of bacon and wood smoke finally worked its way into Sarah's consciousness. She lay very still, not wanting to allow her mind to move beyond the familiar. She would just lie here a few minutes, and when she finally opened her eyes she would be in her bed and all would be normal.

Sarah had never been one to run from her problems, so after about five minutes she slowly opened her eyes. She was lying on a bed, on what could only be a down comforter. There was sunlight streaming through the one curtainless window. She could hear movement on the other side of a plank door.

She slowly sat up and took stock of herself. She was still dressed, but without her jacket. She grabbed her leg, feeling for the pistol that was not there. Her eyes searched the room. They finally located her jacket, hanging from the knob of a large cedar chifforobe, angled in the corner. She continued to search until she found her gun, lying on a small table. The table also held a floral painted wash basin and pitcher. A piece of flannelette had been placed beside the basin.

"I guess these are pretty good accommodations, for eighteen ninety." Sarah spoke aloud, then shook her head at her own foolishness. There was no way that man was going to convince her she had somehow travelled back in time.

She found her boots, side by side, at the foot of the bed. The last thing she remembered was pacing the floor, having a terrible argument with herself, then allowing herself one heck of a crying jag. He must have put her to bed. Well, he was not going to come in here and help her up.

She walked over to the basin and looked at herself in the small round mirror hanging on the wall above the washstand. Good grief! She had a real beauty of a shiner. How the… Oh, she remembered now. Well, at least she was alive. Which was more than could be said for the poor man she had shot. Sarah braced herself with one hand on each side of the wash basin, dropped her head, and closed her eyes.

"Lord, please forgive me. You, better than anyone, know I would never take a life unless it was to save one. I'm not sure how that adds up in your book, Lord, and while I am very sorry that he is dead, I am very grateful to be alive today. Thank you, Jesus. Amen." She washed her face, straightened her hair, knocked a lot of the dust off her jeans, eased on her boots, and headed for the door.

****

Aaron Kramer had not slept much. He finally got up long before daylight. After he'd put the woman to bed last night, he had checked Jeremy for any injuries. Then he had unsaddled Ryker's horse and fed him, along with his mare, who had been patiently waiting in her stall, having found her way home alone from the mountain.

This morning he had re-saddled Ryker's beast, led him about a mile away from the house, then slapped his rear end and sent him running. No point in him being found on his property. It might be a few days, or even weeks, but eventually the law, or someone, would come looking.

He'd washed up at the stream, visited the henhouse, and come in to cook breakfast. Jeremy was seated at the table. He kissed his son on the head, then moved to the stove.

He didn't have much to offer the woman, but it would have to do. He was placing a pan of biscuits on the table when the bedroom door opened. Their eyes met across the room, and his stomach rolled over. Good gosh a-mighty, that eye looked bad. He hoped it didn't feel as bad as it looked.

"Mornin'. How about a cup of coffee?" His voice was still raspy, but the volume was a bit better.

She just nodded and walked to the table. She took a chair across from the boy, smiled, and said, "Good morning," hoping to elicit some sort of response.

"My son's name is Jeremy. He doesn't speak. How do you like your eggs?"

"In my kitchen," she replied.

Aaron raised his chin, and cocked one eyebrow. He hoped she was not gonna start crying again. That fit she pitched last night had torn at him something fierce.

"Don't worry," she said. "We still have a lot to talk about, but there won't be any more displays like last night."

"All right. Let's eat, and then we can talk about yesterday."

He made the eggs over-easy, then handed her a plate with three eggs and the thickest bacon she had ever seen. The biscuits were the size of softballs. He set the jar of honey in the middle of the table.

They sat on each side of the table, and as she picked up a fork, his raspy voice began to pray.

"Dear Lord, I thank you for making it through another night. I thank you for the help you sent me when I needed it most. I thank you that they weren't able to find Jeremy. And Lord, you need to let me know just where I'm to go from here. Amen."

He gave a half smile and handed her the honey jar.

Sarah managed two of the eggs, one of the biscuits, and only one piece of the bacon.

The boy noted her every move as he ate his own breakfast in silence. It was as if she were an insect on a slide, a strange creature he did not understand.

Sarah had not spent a lot of time around kids, but she did know that those this age were usually chatterboxes who never stopped throwing questions at you. So this one's silence was somewhat unnerving.

Aaron stood and gathered the plates. "I guess my over-easy was not to your likin'."

"Oh, no, not that," she was quick to explain. "The eggs were fine. Everything was fine, but it was a bit more than I'm used to eating first thing in the morning."

Aaron placed the dishes in a large pan atop the stove, then covered them with hot water from the kettle. He returned to the table, dropped in his chair, and looked at the woman.

He started to speak but stopped himself to say, "I don't even know your name."

Sarah laughed out loud. "We didn't exactly have time for proper introductions yesterday. My name is Sarah. Sarah Haskins. And your first name is…"

Aaron extended his large hand across the table.

"Aaron, ma'am, Aaron Kramer."

Sarah hesitated for a few seconds, then placed her hand is his.

The touch was electric, and it didn't help that he continued to hold her hand.

"Sarah Haskins, I owe you my life. If you hadn't come along when you did... Well, you know what would have happened."

Sarah looked at the boy. She didn't know if the man had told the boy how they had met, but she sure wasn't going to traumatize a child by telling him his dad had almost died.

Sarah took her hand back but continued to look at Aaron. His dark hair had a hint of curl, causing one lock to fall across his forehead while the rest hung a good inch below his collar. His brown eyes were so dark they reminded her of rich chocolate. He had very broad shoulders, and his rolled-up sleeves revealed strong muscles, with tendons running along his brown forearms.

What he said next tugged her straying mind back to reality.

"Just where did you come from, Sarah?"

"I was hoping you could tell me."

Aaron could see the fear rising in her eyes again.

"All right, what were you doing up on Viking Mountain?"

"I don't know." Her voice had dropped to just above a whisper. "The last thing I remember is sitting in my house, drinking a glass of wine, and staring at a painting of your wife."

"Look, lady, if you don't want to talk about it, fine. But don't be talking foolishness," he snapped.

"I don't know what else to tell you, dammit! There is a painting hanging on the wall in my house. My uncle said it had been in the family for several generations. It is of a woman standing in a forest. She is wearing a beaded dress and a snake bracelet."

If Sarah had not been so upset herself, she would have paid attention to the odd look on Aaron's face and seen that the boy had gone completely white, as if all the blood had left his little body.

"She has a white streak in her hair, and she is holding out her hand to a freaking huge, twelve-point buck."

Aaron leapt up, knocking over his chair. He stormed around the table, grabbed Sarah by the arm, and started dragging her toward a closed door.

"What the hell are you doing?" Sarah tried to jerk her arm free, but he had a death grip that was going to leave some bruises.

Aaron kicked the door open, as he now had both hands on her shoulders. He all but threw her into the room.

Sarah staggered, trying to keep her footing, as she stumbled up against a chest at the foot of a big bed. A bed.

Sarah instantly reached full panic mode. She caught her balance, and spun around to face Aaron.

"If you plan on putting me on that bed, I'm warning you now, mister, you're gonna have to kill me first."

Aaron was stunned. "What the hell..." He froze in the middle of the room. "You don't think I was gonna..."

Well, hell, from the look on her face, that was

exactly what she thought.

"Lady, that is the furthest thing from my mind. Turn around and look at that wall."

Sarah turned warily, keeping him in her peripheral vision.

"Oh, my Lord." All thought of fighting left Sarah with that utterance.

There on the wall was Uncle Fred's painting—the woman, and the stag in the forest. It looked newer and brighter. It was in a different frame, but it was the same painting.

"Now tell me where you've seen this painting. When have you been in my home?"

Sarah turned to face Aaron. He was angry, and she was more than just a little afraid.

The boy was standing in the doorway, watching her as if he too was waiting on her answer.

"Are you in on this thing with Taggart?" he demanded.

Sarah was shaking her head slowly. "Look, I don't know who Taggart is. I don't know how you got this painting. Mister, I don't even know what year it is, so just back off and give me a minute to think!"

His voice was still raspy, but he had regained all his volume.

"Hell, woman. I'm trying to tell you. That is *my* painting. I painted it right after my wife died two years ago," he shouted.

They stood there staring at each other, the air around them still sizzling from the heat of their arguments.

Sarah wilted under the weight of her confusion. She dropped down on the chest and turned frightened eyes to Aaron.

"I think I may be losing my mind."

Aaron wiped a hand across his eyes. He was usually such a calm, steady man. Hell, he couldn't remember the last time he had raised his voice to anyone, least of all a woman.

He gave a soft chuckle. "Well, it hasn't been what you'd call normal for either one of us lately, right?"

Sarah was so relieved to see he was through yelling, for now, that her eyes filled with tears. She swiped angrily at them and jumped up from the chest.

"I need some air. And I need a bathroom. Now."

Aaron nodded. "The small building out back has a tub and a pitcher-pump, but I warn you, that water comes right up from under the mountain and is mighty cold."

Sarah stood there a moment before it dawned on her that he literally meant a room to bathe in.

"No, I mean yes, I'll need a bath later, but right now I need to relieve myself."

"Oh. In that case, out the front door, to your left, and you'll see it down the path."

As Sarah moved toward the door, she glanced at the boy. He was standing just outside the bedroom. As she approached him, he held out his small hand. He was clutching several crumpled pages, obviously ripped from a catalog. It took her a moment to understand how precious was this offering.

The man and the boy just looked at each other. They could hear her maniacal laughter all the way to the outhouse.

When she returned, she found Aaron on the front porch. He held a cup of coffee in each hand. He handed her one of them and then seated himself on the bench, leaving her the bentwood rocker.

"I think we better take some time to talk, maybe get to know each other better. Maybe it'll help us figure out what's going on."

"All right," Sarah agreed. "You go first." She sat back in the rocker and waited. She could see the boy. He was sitting under a tree, out of earshot. He held something in his lap and appeared to be stroking it.

Aaron gazed out across the gently sloping meadow. Where to start?

"The woman in the painting is my wife, Anna. Or she would have been, if we had actually married. Her real name was Ai`yana. It means 'eternal blossom' to the Cherokee. My father and uncle put their money together and bought this place after the war. I guess I was about five or six when they made it back. Pa had been wounded in the back and never quite recovered his health. He died when I was ten. I helped my Uncle Silas build this cabin. I had an eighth-grade teacher who wanted me to take art lessons over in Asheville, but there was no money for that kind of foolishness, and besides, Uncle Silas was a lot older than my pa, and he needed help around here. So I just naturally drifted into raising and training horses." He stopped speaking and looked over at Sarah.

"Some folks say I have a real quiet nature that soothes the animals." He grinned.

Sarah laughed with him. "Like I'm gonna believe that, after the shouting match we had earlier."

Aaron took a sip of coffee, and continued. "Uncle Silas died when I was eighteen, and Mama moved back east, to live with her aging sister."

"A few years later, I was up the mountain, doing some hunting, back in the winter of eighty-two, when I came up on this huge stag. He was carrying what looked like a twelve-point rack. He was just standing in an open spot. I got a good bead on him and was about to squeeze the trigger when someone stepped between me and him. Scared the daylights out of me." He stopped talking and stared at the meadow for a while.

Sarah was about to ask what happened when he started again.

"I could see it was a woman. She had the longest, blackest hair I'd ever seen. She stretched out a hand toward the stag, and I thought, 'Good lord a-mercy, he'll kill her.' But he didn't. He just walked over to her, and she laid her hand on his head, between those huge horns, and he just acted like he was familiar with her. I was frozen to the spot. After a while, he turned and walked away from her, and then she looked right at me. She'd known I was there all along."

Aaron set his cup down on the porch and looked at Sarah. "That's when I knew she was not like the rest of us."

A shiver ran down Sarah's back. That was such an odd thing to say, but before she could ask what he meant, he started again.

"She walked right up to me and smiled. She had the darkest blue eyes, and there was that white stripe in her hair. She said she was lost, and could I give her shelter. She never left. We had our son two years later. I never asked where she came from, and she never spoke of it. Oh, there were signs, but I chose to ignore them. She used to tell Jeremy he was a descendant of the Thunderers. The Cherokee believe these are the controllers of thunder and lightning, that they can 'walk the skies.' Their animal totem is the stag, or a-ha-wi. She would know things without being told. She could sense things before they happened."

He turned to Sarah. "You see, like you, I sometimes think I'm losing my mind. To this day, I believe she knew she'd be gone when I got home from that trip. She held me a little tighter and longer as I was saying goodbye. She whispered in my ear. She said, 'Time is no barrier for love.' 'Course I had no idea what she meant. Still don't."

Sarah noticed he was very matter of fact about it, as if he had adjusted to his loss. If there was one thing Sarah understood, it was loss.

"So," she said, "why are people trying to kill you?"

"Taggart got onto some wild story about iron on my property, and he thinks I ought to just sell him the place and move on."

"So what's keeping you here?"

"Maybe Jeremy, I'm not sure. I just know it's not the right time. Every so often, when I feel like I might want to move on, I'll see that stag. He always stares at me, like he's saying, 'Hold on, something good is coming.' And I just keep holding on. Crazy, right?"

Sarah smiled a sad smile. "No, not crazy. We all have to hold on to something or we'll be lost. What is Jeremy holding on to?"

Aaron turned to face her, and the pain in his eyes was so intense her heart ached for him.

"I left to go pick up some horses in Wilmington. I was only gone for five days. When I got back, there was no one here. The place was in shambles, furniture tossed everywhere. Our closest neighbor is about four miles away, so I started there. She had Jeremy. Said he must have showed up sometime in the night. Her old hound never made a sound. She went out to feed the chickens that morning and found Jeremy and the hound curled up, keeping each other warm. When she tried to question the boy, she understood that something was bad wrong 'cause he wouldn't speak. He cried, but never made a sound. He's been that way ever since. We have no idea what he might have witnessed or how he escaped. Anna was never seen again."

"Aaron, I am so sorry." She looked out across the meadow and met Jeremy's gaze. It was as if the child could sense what they were talking about.

Aaron noted the direction of her gaze.

"It takes a little getting used to. It would almost seem as if he can read your mind, sometimes." Aaron paused, as he watched his son. "All right, Sarah Haskins, so what is your story?"

Sarah told him of losing her parents early and of being raised by her aunt and uncle. How her marriage had fallen apart, and how she'd lost the only two people she had left to love. And then she told him about going to Anna's Gifts and Notions, about the beautiful woman with the dark blue eyes and the white stripe in her hair, about trying on the snake bangle but then settling for the arrowhead.

When she got to that part, she stuck her hand in her shirt, and drew out the rawhide ribbon. She held the piece out for Aaron to see. She was not prepared for what happened next.

Aaron's eyes widened in shock. His knuckles whitened as he gripped the edge of the bench. He slowly raised a hand to his throat and removed a rawhide ribbon from his shirt. There, on the end of the leather strip, hung an arrowhead carved from a piece of Tennessee Paint Rock agate.

"Well, imagine that," Sarah said sarcastically. "Where did you get yours? No, don't tell me. Anna gave it to you, right?"

"Just before I left to go to Wilmington."

Sarah had no words left. The whole set of circumstances was bizarre; she was beginning to believe they were both crazy.

"Aaron, last night when I asked you what the date was, you told me the year of our Lord eighteen ninety, right?"

He still looked pale when he nodded yes.

"Well, when I fell asleep night before last, it was the year of our Lord two thousand sixteen. Do you understand what I'm telling you? Somehow, in a way that neither one of us can explain, I left my home, in my time, and arrived here to save you, in yours. Only one hundred twenty-six years lies somewhere between us."

Chapter Four

It was the end of September. The nights were a little cooler and the days a little shorter.

Aaron had told her that Jeremy always enjoyed accompanying him on early morning hunting trips, before she arrived. But since Sarah had appeared, he was never far away from her. While he never spoke, he seemed to anticipate her every need. Often he would walk into the room only to hand her something she had been looking for, as if he could read her mind.

They had settled into a peaceful routine. Aaron would do breakfast, and Sarah would do supper.

This morning, Aaron had awakened her early.

"I'm sorry to have to wake you so early, but I need to leave before daylight if I'm gonna find something for supper, and I didn't want you to wake up and think we had abandoned you," Aaron apologized, as he placed a pan of biscuits on the table. "Jeremy got up and put his jacket and gloves on the table, so I'm thinking he's going hunting with me."

Sarah smiled at the boy as she said, "Well, that's real nice of you fellows. I'll have a little private time." Did she actually see a response in Jeremy's eyes, or was it just her imagination? "If you can bring home supper, the least I can do is get up early. I'll be using the wash house today, so I'll need to get an early start anyway."

Sarah sipped the strong coffee she had learned to enjoy. "By the way, there is very little in the way of 'fixin's' left in the root cellar."

Aaron looked at her over the top of his tin cup. He was still amazed every morning that this beautiful woman was under his roof. He couldn't explain where she'd come from, but he remembered to thank the Lord every night.

"I guess it's about time for me to introduce you to Granny."

"Your grandmother lives near?"

Aaron laughed. "She's not really my grandmother. She's the grandmother for anyone who knows her. She and her husband never had children of their own. He died from a copperhead bite a few years back. I finished up a couple of projects he'd had going around the place, so Granny has been trying to feed me ever since. She always plants a garden big enough to feed an army, so she sends enough food to get me through 'til the spring."

Aaron and Jeremy left right after breakfast. Aaron was pleased to have Jeremy with him. The boy could sit motionless for hours if that was what it took to find food. Aaron found a clearing with signs of turkey scratching. It was not quite full-on daybreak. He motioned for Jeremy to sit under a large oak. Aaron would make his way around the clearing so that he would not be looking into the sun when it rose.

An hour after daybreak, his patience was justified, and Aaron shot a large tom turkey. Sarah would probably have to stew the bird instead of roast him, but it would make for a few meals.

Aaron was making his way back to Jeremy, when

he froze in his tracks. There, several yards away, was Jeremy—with the stag. Jeremy was rubbing the animal's ears. Aaron's first thought was that if the thing had been a cat, he could have heard the purring from where he stood, such was the look of contentment on its face.

Suddenly the stag raised his head in acknowledgement of Aaron's presence.

Jeremy turned toward his father, and Aaron could see the sheen of tears on his small face.

Aaron's worst fear was that the stag had hurt Jeremy, and he was about to break into a run when Jeremy slowly shook his head from side to side. Aaron forced himself to be still. He watched as Jeremy laid his head against the beast's side for a moment. Then the animal turned and faded into the early morning mist.

Aaron was unsure what to say when he got to Jeremy. He knelt in front of the boy and slowly wiped the tears from his face, and though neither of them spoke aloud, the sharing of the experience drew each of their hearts closer than they had been in some time. Aaron lifted the child and carried him close to his chest as he made his way home. He had not gone far when the sound of soft snoring in his ear told him the child was sleeping soundly. Aaron held him a little tighter and thanked the Lord. He was not sure what his thanks centered around. He was just grateful for the feeling of peace and comfort that washed over him as he held his sleeping child.

It was near noon when Aaron broke through the forest east of the cabin. There in the late morning sun was a sight to behold.

Sarah had found a comfortable spot in some tall

grass. She was wrapped in a blanket and had allowed it to drop from her shoulders while she raked a comb through her still damp hair.

She was angled away from him, and while she could not see him, he could see enough of her to warrant a sudden response from his body. As she tossed her hair over one shoulder, he had a clear line of sight to the curve of her exposed breast.

While the artist in him admired the curvature of her, from shoulder to hip, the man in him remembered how warm and soft a woman's flesh could feel. He didn't want to embarrass her, but he couldn't stand there all day, and Jeremy was sure to wake.

He turned his back to her and called out softly, "Sarah, I'm coming in. You might want to cover yourself."

Sarah jerked her head around and was glad to find he was turned away from her. She scrambled to her feet and readjusted the blanket to a more useful position.

"Sorry. You can turn around now. I must have taken longer than I realized in the bath. That water was frigid. Next time I'll carry the tub into my room and heat some water on the stove." Sarah could hear herself babbling, but she couldn't seem to stop. "I would have washed some of your clothes, as well, but you didn't leave any out for me, and I didn't want to prowl around in your room."

Aaron could see the flush of color in her face as she continued to run on. He almost smiled. While it was a warm day, he didn't think the flush had anything to do with the weather. He stopped a few feet away and waited for her to run down.

Sarah finally met his gaze. His eyes never strayed

from her face. As she lowered hers, they moved past the child he was carrying, and there was clear, visible proof of his reaction to her nudity.

She immediately raised her eyes—and froze when she met his gaze. She could not think of a single thing to say.

Aaron smiled slowly. "I won't apologize, Sarah. You are a beautiful woman, and it would be real unnatural for me to just ignore the sight of you."

Her face was near flaming now. "Don't be silly. We're both adults. There's no need for apologies. I'll just go see how dry my clothes are now."

As she turned toward the cabin, he dropped the turkey and caught her arm. Sarah grabbed the front of the blanket, holding it secure.

"Sarah, I was just going to say that Anna's clothes are all in a trunk in my room. I mean, just in case yours are not dry yet."

She stood very still. The feel of his rough hand around her upper arm was causing her mind to work a little slowly.

"Clothes? In a trunk?"

Aaron ran his hand down her arm until he was circling her wrist. He held her arm out to one side. "I think you carry a pound or two more, but I'm sure they'll do."

Sarah's whole arm was tingling now, and she needed to move before she made a fool of herself.

"Thank you. I'll just go see what I can find," she blurted out before she practically ran to the cabin.

"Take your time," Aaron called out. "After I get Jeremy settled, and clean this turkey, I think I'll make use of the washhouse myself."

Sarah rummaged through the trunk quietly, trying not to picture Aaron in the washhouse.

She got flustered all over again. Good grief, the child was asleep on the cot at the foot of his father's bed, and here she was letting her imagination get the best of her.

She finally found a dark blue serge skirt, and a pale yellow blouse that fit her. The skirt swept the tops of her bare feet, and the blouse was a little snugger than she would have liked, but at least she was covered. She laid aside a green shirtwaist dress for tomorrow and was closing the lid on the trunk when footsteps stopped at the door.

Sarah looked up. A shirtless Aaron was standing there with water dripping from his tousled hair. His muscle definition had been lost under the long-sleeved shirts he always wore, but every tendon and curve was evident now, and Sarah allowed her eyes to take in every inch of them, until his voice caught her attention.

"Sarah, I'm a fairly well-disciplined man, and I would never force myself on a woman. However, it would be a lot easier for me to stick to my principles if you could just stop lookin' at me with those hungry eyes," he said softly.

Sarah's mind snapped to attention at his words. Good heavenly days, she was acting like some awe-stricken, hormone-crazed teenager.

"Supper will be ready in an hour," she snapped. Then, with head held high, she marched her barefoot self into the kitchen.

She had located a quart jar of tomatoes, an onion, and a rutabaga. She could make that work with the turkey hanging on the back porch. As she peeled the onion and rutabaga, she let her mind wander. If she was to go on living in this house—as if she had other options—she was going to have to set some boundaries. The sight of a shirtless Aaron had reminded her just how long it had been since she'd been intimate with a man.

True, she wasn't an innocent young girl anymore, but she did have morals. Her work schedule had prevented her from attending church on a regular basis, but you didn't have to be in a pew every Sunday to know right from wrong. And it would be wrong for her to just allow herself to fall into a loose relationship with a man, especially with a child in the house. Besides, she wasn't about to give up her independence, not ever again.

****

Greeneville, Tennessee, October 2016

Frank Kramer checked his watch. Yeah, he'd make it with minutes to spare. He hated leaving Lisa with all the stuff that still needed sorting after the move, but it wouldn't look good to be late taking on his first case in Greeneville. He liked this town. It suited the life he and Lisa wanted for little Frank. Good schools, God-fearing people, a slower vibe, and the Lord alone knew that anything was better than New York, he thought to himself as he entered the Greeneville sheriff's offices.

He stopped at the front desk. "Agent Frank Kramer to see Sheriff Lassiter." He smiled at the young deputy.

Five minutes later he was shaking hands with a barrel-chested man in his late fifties.

"Thank you, Agent Kramer, for being on time. I've got a lot on my plate today, and I'm glad to be turning this one over to you. Are you familiar with the story?"

"To tell you the truth, sir, I just got settled in the new office in the courthouse yesterday. Before that, I was moving my wife and five-year-old son into our new home. I haven't been briefed on this case at all."

"All right, then," Lassiter drawled as he slid a folder across the wide, glass-topped desk. "I'll give you a quick rundown, but everything we have is in that folder."

"Greeneville is a relatively small town, and if you've lived here a while, people get to know you. Well, we've got an employee that's gone missing. The girl was raised right here in Greene County, by an older aunt and uncle. Poor kid lost her parents in a crash over in Gatlinburg when she was a little thing. Sarah was a great student and would have gone on to do great things in college, but her aunt took sick. So she hired on to work for me, so she could be close to home. The girl was a damned fine dispatcher, levelheaded and calm no matter what was thrown at her, and she always had a smile on her face. She did have a couple of rough years. She married one of my deputies. The boy wasn't from around these parts. He turned out to be an idiot and got caught up with a high-school kid. Anyway, he was fired and is still doing time. But here is the problem. Sarah Haskins left work on August fourteenth to start a three-week vacation. She hasn't been seen or heard from since. When she didn't show back up for work, her supervisor sent a deputy out to her farm. She lives alone, on twenty-some odd acres. Her truck was there. House was secured from the inside. One of the girls in dispatch told the deputy there was a key in a birdhouse or something—anyway, he entered and found nothing but a bottle of sangria and an empty glass in the den.

No signs of a struggle. Everything secured." The sheriff turned to gaze out his window.

Agent Kramer could see the sheriff was truly concerned about this employee. He picked up the folder and opened it. The first page was an eight-by-ten color photograph of the woman in question. Kramer was forty years old; he had been an agent with the Bureau for fifteen years. Occasionally, he might have trouble recalling a name, but he never forgot a face. And he knew this one. He couldn't say where, or when, but he'd seen this face before... He was so deep in concentration the sheriff had to speak to him twice.

"Excuse me?" Agent Kramer apologized as he closed the folder.

"I said, can you take this on? I know it's practically a cold case now, but my folks have run out of leads, and it has caused a lot of tension and concern in my dispatch center. This girl just up and disappeared, and we need help."

Frank Kramer was getting that feeling, the one that began deep in his chest and always meant he was onto something odd.

He stood and extended his hand to the sheriff. "I will give this my full attention, sir. I'll keep you posted."

"If you have any questions, call Sergeant Harper. His people put the file together."

Sheriff Lassiter watched the agent walk across the parking lot.

He hoped that boy was good. They hated to give up on such a sweet girl, but she had just vanished into thin air.

****

Viking Valley, October 1890

Aaron was concerned. Over the last several days, Sarah had become more and more withdrawn. He would find her sitting quietly, gazing into the distance. He wondered if she was pining for the life she'd had ripped away. Several times he'd had to call her name twice before she responded. He recognized that she was losing the will to participate in this life, the here and now.

He recognized it because he had slipped into that empty place when he lost Anna. It was months before he could accept that she was gone and that he had to keep on living, for his son. He had to do something to draw her back from the edge.

"Sarah, it's time you met Granny." He smiled across the breakfast table. While they had settled into a comfortable companionship, there were times he had to take a long walk in the cool night air, or even a dip in the cold creek, to cool down. Sarah was a beautiful woman, and he had been alone for two years. He was often glad that Jeremy was there, acting as an unknowing buffer between him and his growing feelings for Sarah.

Sarah accepted the fact that she had been difficult to live with lately. She was wrestling with a couple of serious issues. On the one hand, she was having to live a totally different, though not unfamiliar, lifestyle. She had already sent prayers of thanks up to her aunt and uncle for insisting that she learn how to live on a farm. Washing clothes and dishes by hand was not the easiest thing, but it was not the worst. And while she missed her co-workers and her job, not having to deal with the pain in the lives of those who called in was a relief.

That was one of the issues she was trying to work through.

The second issue was on a totally different level. She spent way more time than she should thinking about how it would feel to wake up beside Aaron after a night of wild lovemaking. But never again would Sarah make the mistake of thinking hormonal urges were strong enough to be the foundation for a loving relationship. She had learned to live without love rather than take the chance of being hurt again. But this man...this man could light a flame in her with a sideways glance, and it frightened her. And besides, there was Jeremy. The two of them were developing an understanding. It was fragile, and she would never want to do anything that might hurt the child.

"Well, it's the middle of October, and if I'd known in early summer that I would have another mouth to feed, I would have put in a garden. But it's too late for that now, so we're gonna do the next best thing. Granny is about four miles west of here. She was so grateful for my help when her husband passed on, she now makes it her mission in life to can enough food for us to eat well all winter."

"Oh. Just how old is this neighbor that takes such good care of you?" Sarah asked in what she hoped was a teasing voice.

Aaron laughed aloud. "I told you, she's probably ninety. Her husband was a spry ol' fella. A good builder, and strong as an ox. Granny has slowed a little since his death but still has more energy than most grown men.

"Even though she is alone now, she just keeps on gardening and putting up enough food to feed a good-sized family. She'll be glad I've got another mouth to feed. It'll make her feel needed. And besides, she hasn't seen Jeremy in a while. She was there for him when his mama first disappeared. And he would love to see ol' Red."

While Sarah worried every day that she was an unexpected burden for Aaron, she couldn't help enjoying the warm feeling she got inside when he spoke as if she was his responsibility. It was new and exciting to think that she was not alone anymore; that someone was happy to look out for her. She smiled back at him over the rim of her coffee cup.

Aaron swallowed hard. He didn't think Sarah understood what it did to him when she got that dreamy-eyed look. He'd been talking to the Lord about this for weeks now. He'd asked Him for patience, and if he couldn't have enough patience to let her make the first move, then he asked to be filled with gentleness, 'cause it was just a matter of time before he made love to this woman.

"You clear the table, and Jeremy and I will saddle the horses. Then we'll ride over and meet Granny."

An hour or so later, Sarah could make out a small cabin in the distance. As they approached, it was clear to see that a large field had been picked clean, leaving a wide variety of vines, stalks, and bushes to die and dry in the autumn sun.

Sarah shook her head. "That has to be at least two acres of garden. It took some serious work to plant, grow, and harvest that much stuff."

Aaron laughed. "Wait until you see Granny."

As they neared the cabin, a dog began to howl. Sarah looked around and spotted an old, faded red hound hauling himself to a standing position. She could see his muzzle was turning gray and his stance was a little wobbly, but he was doing his best to maintain his reputation as a guard dog.

They brought the horses to a standstill just as Granny stepped to the screen door.

It took her a moment to recognize Aaron as she peered out from under the wide brim of an old poke bonnet.

"Lord, child! I was beginnin' to think you had passed on and nobody had told ol' Granny. Well, git on down and come on in. I got some fresh pie, just out of the oven. Jeremy's favorite, huckleberry." The little woman turned and disappeared back into the cabin.

Aaron turned a grinning face to Sarah. "Pie. Oh, boy, am I ready."

Sarah laughed out loud. "You sound like a ten-year-old who's in for a great treat."

"Just wait until you taste this pie! Jeremy will tell you it's the best thing you've ever had in your mouth. Right, son?"

Sarah looked at Jeremy. He never cracked a grin, but nodded solemnly, as if this pie was a matter on par with life after death.

She followed the boys into the little home, where she was amazed at the interior. It was spotless, neat as a pin, and just plain homey. Lovely chintz curtains covered the windows, and hand-embroidered pillows adorned the horsehair sofa and chairs. There were lovely, lacy, crocheted scarves on all the tabletops. It was easy to see what occupied Granny during the winter months.

The little woman had removed her bonnet,

revealing the thick coil of hair atop her head was pure white.

Granny turned from the stove and stopped abruptly. "Well, you've found a friend, I see. Come on over here, honey, and let old Granny get a look at you."

Sarah was glad she had on the green shirtwaist dress. She didn't think Granny would have approved of her jeans.

"Now, ain't you a beauty? Child, you need to be wearin' a hat. That old sun will dry up your beautiful face afore you know it, and you'll end up lookin' like an old raisin, just like me." The old woman cackled at her own joke.

The pie was scrumptious, and when Sarah caught the grin on Aaron's face as she asked for seconds, she just stuck out her purple tongue at him.

They had a long visit with Granny. Jeremy sat outside under a massive black walnut tree with old Red's head in his lap. Once, when Sarah peeked out the door to check on him, she could have sworn his mouth was moving, as if he was speaking to the dog.

Granny insisted on them taking the small cart home. She filled it with jars of vegetables and some fruit jams, nestled in several old quilts. By the time Aaron attached the cart to his saddle, the sun was dropping below the mountaintops, filling the valley with shadows that would melt into darkness in less than an hour.

They had traveled only a hundred yards or so when Sarah's horse reared and then bucked, snorting and screaming. Sarah was caught completely off guard and was sent flying over his head. In the hope of slowing her descent, she flailed at thin air. Just before she slammed into the ground, she recognized the source of his fear. She had no time to process what might happen before she landed, face down, on the copperhead.

All the breath was knocked from her lungs upon impact, and she was still struggling to refill them when Aaron reached her side.

"Careful..." Her voice whistled, as she sucked air. "Snake."

Aaron recoiled in shock as he turned Sarah onto her back in time to see the copperhead slither quickly into the growing dusk.

"Damn! Did he get you, Sarah? Are you okay?"

Sarah's dress was tangled around her thighs, and as Aaron was about to lower it, he spotted the two little circles of blood just below her right knee.

"Ah, hell, Sarah, you've been bitten."

She was still trying to regulate her breathing when his words worked their way into her mind. Her first thought was to thank the Lord that it was she who'd been thrown, not Jeremy.

Before the fear had time to set in, Aaron had scooped her up into his arms and was headed back to Granny's at a dead run.

Time was now their enemy, so he yelled as he ran. "Granny! Snakebite!"

He barely noticed, as he entered the cabin, that the old lady had ripped the tablecloth from the big pine plank table. He didn't even see the shattered dishes on the floor. Granny was holding a jug of 'shine in one hand, old Doc Harold's suction cup and a straight razor in the other.

Sarah's mind was working overtime. The odds of her surviving were slim to none, but she hadn't won all those awards for nothing. They were for being able to use her head under pressure.

As Aaron placed her on the tabletop, she grabbed his arm.

"Listen to me. This is very important. You're gonna do everything you can to get as much poison out of me as possible, but no matter what you do, some will get through. We must slow it down so my body can work to destroy it. You need to knock me out."

The look on Aaron's face said he thought she was already delirious.

"Damn it, listen to me! If I am unconscious, my heart will slow down, and the poison will also. Just take your fist and knock me out. If you don't, I will probably die! Aaron, just do what I tell you. I know more about this kind of thing than you do."

She had a death grip on Aaron's left arm. When her words finally broke through his panicked mind, he understood their underlying meaning: *I know things from my time that you don't know.*

Their eyes met, each holding so many yet-unspoken things.

Aaron placed a hand under her head and lowered his mouth to hers hungrily as if he had to experience, in just one kiss, any future they might have. It was a kiss like neither had ever experienced before—hot and desperate, yet full of hope.

And then he hit her. Jeremy was standing by the table like a white marble statue. That was the vision planted in her mind as she lost consciousness.

Chapter Five

Aaron was grateful that Sarah had been unconscious during the cutting and the bloodletting, but now he wanted her to wake up. He had spent at least half an hour rubbing Sarah's leg in a downward direction, forcing the blood from the two wounds. And now both he and Granny were starting to worry that he had hit her too hard.

Aaron could still hear Granny's cry.

"What in blue blazes are you doin'? Are you crazy?" The old woman had looked as if she might hit him over the head with one of her many skillets hanging above the woodstove. He couldn't explain to Granny why he'd knocked Sarah out, because he wasn't real sure himself. He only knew that Sarah was sure he needed to, and that was good enough for him. The only thing worse than Granny's anger had been Jeremy's fear.

Aaron had looked up from the bloodletting to see the child standing by the table. His eyes had been round as saucers. He'd been trembling as he held onto a chair. Once Granny had declared Aaron had to stop before he bled Sarah to death, he'd cleaned his hands, scooped Jeremy into his arms, and held the boy until he'd fallen into a fitful sleep, and the child now lay on the sofa.

Aaron was jerked from his thoughts by a soft moan. He was immediately on his knees beside the bed.

Sarah wanted to open her eyes, but she could feel a terrible, throbbing pain in her face and was afraid to let in any light. A pungent odor kept teasing her nose. She moaned again, and someone bathed her face with a cool cloth. She blinked a couple of times, then forced her eyelids apart. Her vision was a little blurred, but she could make out the look of fear on Aaron's face.

"Hello," she whispered. "How am I doing?"

"You're alive. I bled you enough to scare Granny into threatening my life if I didn't stop. How do you feel?"

"Like I sparred a few rounds with Ali and lost."

Aaron's heart clenched. She was delirious.

Sarah closed her eyes and smiled. "Like some big strong horse trainer clobbered me with a right hook."

"Oh. Sarah, I am so sorry."

"Shush. You probably saved my life. Besides, I told you to, so I can't very well blame the headache on you."

Aaron wiped her face again. "Granny cleaned the straight razor, and your leg, with moonshine. I kept the cuts under a half inch, and if it was possible to wash out the poison with the blood flow, then you should be okay. After Granny's husband died, old Doc Harold gave her a suction cup to keep. She used that first, and then I rubbed your legs for near a half hour, forcing the blood to flow, until Granny said I was gonna bleed you to death. So I stopped. She said she would stitch the cuts up tomorrow, but she wanted to make sure they had stopped draining first. She bathed them with apple cider vinegar, and she swears that will lessen the chance of the bite site becoming putrid and dying."

"Well, it sounds like the two of you have done all

you could. Now if only I had a couple of Xanax."

There was instant confusion on Aaron's face, and she realized he had no idea what she was talking about.

She smiled. "Something to make me sleep, so my heartbeat stays slower than normal."

Aaron returned the smile. "Well, if you think you're woman enough to handle it, there's some 'shine left in the jug."

Sarah was not much of a drinker, just the occasional glass of wine, but if the 'shine, as Aaron called it, would put her to sleep, so be it.

"Okay, I'll take a glass of Granny's elixir."

It took her about half an hour, with much coughing and sputtering, to down a glassful. She finally got to the "I've had too much to drink and don't care what I say" state.

Aaron could see she was just about ready to pass out. He was bathing her face again when she grasped his hand.

"You know what would help me sleep?"

Aaron grinned as he brushed her hair out of her face. Her speech was slurred, and she could barely keep her eyes open.

"What, Sarah, what would help you sleep?"

"You could climb in here an' hol' me in those big ol' arms o' yours. Ya know, spoon me, from behind. I bet I'd go right ta sleep."

She was far enough gone that she didn't hear his sharp intake of breath or see the passion flare in Aaron's eyes.

"So you think that would help?"

"Uh-huh." Her voice was barely a whisper now.

Aaron pulled off his boots and climbed across

Sarah. He stretched his long body out behind hers.

Sarah snuggled backwards until they were touching, top to bottom.

Aaron crossed his arm over her, and eased a little closer. This. This was what had kept him awake at night. Imagining just how this would feel.

Sarah took Aaron's large hand in hers, and placed it on her breast.

While his blood surged and his heart raced, hers slowed to a snail's pace, and she drifted into a deep, alcohol-induced sleep.

Aaron dozed as Jeremy stood in the shadowed doorway, the smallest of smiles lighting his young face.

****

Aaron woke with a start. He hadn't meant to sleep, just comfort Sarah.

It was the heat that woke him. She was burning up, and while he was soaked in sweat, she was dry and hot to the touch.

"Granny," he yelled.

By the time he had climbed over Sarah to stand beside the bed, the little woman had rushed in with a lantern.

"What is it, boy? Is she awake?"

"No, she's still out, but she is hot to the touch. Is she supposed to have a fever?" There was abject fear in his voice, and when Granny looked up into his face, she could see her own reflected in his eyes. This man, who had been so kind to her, and who had lost so much already, might be about to lose again.

"Now, calm down and let ol' Granny think. We must cool her down or she won't make it. Let me grab some blankets, and the lantern. You carry her. We'll take her up to the spring."

Aaron knew Granny had a spring on her property, but he'd never seen it. He followed behind the woman as she moved up a narrow path into the forest, with Jeremy trailing behind him. Granny finally stopped and hung the lantern on a pole.

Aaron could see the light dancing across the black water. It looked to be about eight feet across. Someone had set rocks in a circle and dug around the spring, creating a good-sized pool.

"That's about five feet deep in the middle, son, so you'll just have to carry her in and dunk her in the water."

Aaron hadn't bothered with his boots when he jumped from the bed, so now he stepped over the rim of rocks and eased out into the pool. His body gave a shudder at the onslaught of cold water, and he was immediately covered in goosebumps.

"Put her in slow, boy. She might wake up and fight ya."

Aaron slowly moved toward the center of the pool, allowing the water to rise an inch or so with each step. By the time he reached the middle, the water was up to his chest, and only Sarah's head was above the water line.

Aaron could see her face in the lantern's light. Her brows were furrowed in a grimace, as if her body was angry at the intrusion into her deep sleep. After a while, she began to moan occasionally, and then she began to whimper.

Granny nodded. "That's it, boy, just hold onto her. The cold is startin' to work."

The cold was working on Aaron as well. His bare

feet were beginning to go numb, and his arms were trembling, not from Sarah's weight, which was supported by the water, but from the biting cold of the spring itself.

Sarah was dreaming. She was afraid, but of what? Her alcohol-fogged mind could not sort out her fear. She wanted to wake up, but something kept weighing her down; something was trying to take her to a dark place. From the darkness that surrounded her, whispered a sound so sweet she wanted to cry. It was a woman singing. Sarah could see her now. The woman was standing in the forest, her back to Sarah and her arms raised to the heavens as she sang. The melody was soothing to Sarah, even though she couldn't make out the words. They were in a language unknown to her. And then the woman turned. She had shiny black hair except for the wide white streak on one side. She smiled at Sarah and seemed to float toward her. The woman touched Sarah's head, and the touch was cool and comforting. The woman crooned softly to Sarah.

"It is not time for you to pass over. You are where you are meant to be. The heart knows nothing of time. Much love and happiness await you, if you accept it." The woman began to fade from Sarah's dream.

"Don't go, tell me more."

Aaron was startled when Sarah spoke aloud.

"No, don't leave," she mumbled weakly.

"Sarah, honey, open your eyes. I'm not going to leave you. Sarah, wake up."

She managed to open her eyes. It was dark, except for the weak light of a lantern nearby. She looked up into Aaron's face, slowly becoming aware that he was holding her in his arms and that they were both wet and shivering from the cold. She raised both arms to encircle Aaron's neck and brought his face close to hers.

"Why are we bathing in the middle of the night?" she whispered.

Aaron threw back his head and laughed, even as tears of gratitude ran down his cheeks.

****

Sarah woke suddenly, clutching the quilt to her chest. She looked wildly around the room. It was not familiar to her, but the smell of coffee and bacon assured her all must be well. Slowly her memory returned. She rolled to her side and let her mind sort things out at its own pace. She could feel the tightness in her leg, indicating a swelling, and she could remember Aaron striking her.

Yes. She'd been bitten by a snake. Even as she remembered this, she felt the stiffness around her right knee, not from the bandage that surrounded it but from the poison, she was sure.

She touched her face. The whole left side ached when she clenched her jaw. That would be from Aaron's right hook. She remembered telling him he must knock her out—and did she imagine it, or did he kiss her then?

And she was not losing her mind. She did wake up to Aaron trying to freeze her to death in a pond.

Ah, this must be Granny's bedroom, then. Yes, they were just leaving the dear woman's home when it happened. She needed to pee. Well, that was a good sign. It seemed she was going to survive the bite.

She threw off the covers, only to discover she was nearly naked. She sat up and inspected her covering.

She was wearing only a man's shirt. A large man's shirt. Ah, there was her dress, hanging over a chair. She swung her legs over the side of the bed and was about to stand when she became aware of Jeremy. He was seated on a small stool at the foot of the bed.

He stood, and she could see that he was holding a night bucket. He extended it toward her.

Sarah smiled. She stood to take the bucket from him, and the whole room began to spin, at first slowly but then picking up the pace. She closed her eyes, thinking that might help, but that only prevented her from seeing the floor rush up to meet her.

Aaron heard the thud and was out of his chair in a flash. He found Jeremy standing over Sarah, who lay unconscious and half naked on the floor. The boy had the night bucket in his hand. He must have just been waiting for Sarah to waken and need it.

Aaron was angered by the conflict of emotions that ran through him. He was filled with guilt by the sight of her face, black and blue where he had struck her. The bandage on her right knee still seeped bloody fluid from the cuts he'd made.

His son was standing over Sarah, his tears showing a fear he could not express, and still Aaron's body had the nerve to react to the beauty of her, lying there with her hair fanned out around her shoulders, the shirt barely concealing her hips. With a grunt of self-disgust, he knelt and scooped her from the floor, placed her gently on the bed, and covered that tempting sight with the sheet.

"Here, try this," Granny said, handing him the bottle of smelling salts.

He was startled by her voice. His mind had been

filled with thoughts of climbing into the bed and holding Sarah until she woke.

He cleared his throat. "Thank you, Granny." He took the small bottle from her and waved it under Sarah's nose.

She in turn began to jerk her head away from the pungent odor, blinking her tearing eyes several times.

"What…where…did I fall?" She finally managed to get out, as she struggled to sit up.

Chapter Six

"Don't worry, Granny, we'll take it slow and easy, but, we've got to get back home. I watered the chickens well, and they have that long run to find bugs once the feed runs out, but I'm sure they're wondering what's going on by now."

"Well, don't you let that poor thing be walkin' around. She needs to stay off that leg for a while."

They'd been at Granny's for four days now, and it was time to go home.

Home. Just thinking the word in her head teased a smile to Sarah's face.

Aaron carried her to her horse and carefully placed her left foot in the stirrup.

"Now, be careful swinging that leg over," he ordered, as he moved to the other side of her horse.

"All right, that's good." He raised her dress and ran his hand slowly up Sarah's leg, pausing at her knee. Then he gently lifted the leg away from the saddle, while he placed a folded lap quilt between Sarah and the saddle.

"How's that?"

When Sarah did not answer, Aaron looked up.

She would've answered him, but his hand slowly stroking up her leg had stolen her breath.

"Did I hurt you, Sarah?"

She could hear the concern in his question. She just

shook her head no. She couldn't very well tell him her leg was on fire—not from the snake bite but from the feel of his calloused hand on her skin.

"All right, if you're ready?"

"Oh, yes. I'm ready. Let's go home." Aaron paused a moment, searching her face for any sign of pain. Her cheeks had a little color, but Granny said the fever was all gone. Must be the moving after so many days in bed.

"Then home it is." He smiled at the sound of those words. Home. With Sarah and Jeremy.

****

"No, ma'am, you sit yourself right back down. Granny would have my head if I let you try to walk to the outhouse. Use the pot I gave you, and I'll empty it."

Sarah was so frustrated she almost growled. "I will not have you, or anyone else, handling my slop bucket."

Aaron sat on the edge of the bed. "Look at me, Sarah."

She had turned away from him in total embarrassment.

"Sarah, I said look at me." He waited.

Sarah finally turned her red face toward him but could not quite meet his gaze. She was looking at the dark hair showing at the unbuttoned neck of his shirt.

Aaron reached out to cup her chin. "Sarah, we're both adults. We've both lived with a mate. While you might wish for me to pretend you don't have bodily functions like the rest of the world, the truth is I know different."

She finally met his gaze, only to realize he was trying his best not to laugh. After a long moment of watching his lips twitch from trying to hold off a smile, Sarah smiled, then burst into laughter.

"All right, all right, I'll use the darn bucket," she conceded. "However, I'm gonna need my share of the catalog, if you please."

****

"Okay, that's the last bucket. Remember, keep your knee dry."

"Yes, 'Mother,' I'll bathe with one leg out of the tub. For crying out loud, quit fussing. I'm fine, my leg is healing nicely, and either you leave me alone and let me use the tub, or I'm walking to the creek. You got that?"

Aaron stood in the doorway, both hands on his hips. He could hear the frustration in her voice. Maybe he was being a little overbearing, but dang it, he'd already lost one woman. Good grief! Where did that come from? This woman did not belong to him. He had no rights where she was concerned.

She was about to ask Aaron why he was still here when she caught the puzzled look on his face. He appeared to be having some sort of inner argument.

Aaron finally shook his head, turned, and closed the door behind himself.

Sarah let out a long sigh. She was tired. Things had been strained between them lately. There seemed to be an underlying tension with a cause she couldn't pinpoint. She didn't like the way they were snapping at each other.

She raised the dress over her head, dropped it on the bed, and moved to the side of the tub. She swung her left foot over the side, then slowly lowered her bottom, being careful not to slosh the water all over the floor. She kept her right leg bent at the knee and hanging over the side.

She looked at the scars now forming just below the right knee. It wasn't pretty, but the mere fact that she had survived the bite was a good indication that the Lord was not finished with her, but why? What was she doing here, in this time, with this man? How did this happen?

Sarah lifted her hair, leaned back against the edge of the tub, and allowed her hair to drop over the tub rim. She closed her eyes and tried to clear her head. Every time she started trying to find the "why" of her situation, she was reduced to tears. She'd always taken care of others, but here, in this time, she had to depend on a man. It wasn't like she could just walk out the door and live on her own. It was eighteen-ninety. Women who were not married lived with family members. Sarah's eyes filled. She had no family. She had accepted that and was okay with it. However, for some reason, it was different here and now. She was no longer content.

That was the problem. She wanted more. She was no longer content to just pass from day to day. That was an existence. Sarah wanted a life. A life full of love, and companionship, and yes, physical pleasures. The tears that had pooled now ran down her cheeks. She could not hold in the small sobs that gathered at the back of her throat.

****

Aaron stood outside the closed door long enough to hear the water splashing. He then poured himself the last of the coffee and headed to the porch.

There were so many questions he needed answered. He'd been through this frustration before. When he'd come home to find Anna missing, he'd railed at God. He'd cried out for answers. And when none came, he moved on with his life. He'd settled into a routine with Jeremy that kept him sane.

And then Sarah had arrived. He'd told the Lord every night since that he was grateful for her. That he understood her coming into his life at that moment was a gift, one he did not deserve. However, now he wanted more. He was no longer satisfied with moving through life with no purpose. He wanted Sarah to be his purpose. He wanted her to belong to him. Oh, not just to satisfy his physical needs, but to laugh with and to share dreams with, to build a life together.

Aaron looked out across the pasture. The one thing he didn't want was for her to feel she had no other choice. She must often think of the life she no longer had access to, and she must surely miss it. He didn't want her to accept a life with him because she had no choice.

He suddenly knew just what he wanted. He wanted Sarah to love him. To want to spend her life with him. He wanted Sarah to choose him.

****

Aaron looked again, just to be sure. Yep, that was a moccasin print. He stood there for several minutes. From the corner of the chicken coop, where he was standing, you could see right in Sarah's window. Someone had been standing there—for a good while, he suspected, as there were lots of scuffed prints. Taggart had a man working for him that was half Cherokee.

From now on, Sarah and Jeremy had to stay near the cabin. No wandering off to pick flowers or talk with the animals. He didn't want to frighten either of them, but this was serious.

Sarah was sewing a loose button on one of Jeremy's shirts when Aaron entered with the full egg basket.

She looked up and smiled at him, then took in the look on his face. She placed the shirt on the table and folded her hands in her lap.

"What's wrong?"

Jeremy raised his head. He was sitting at Sarah's feet, weaving pine needles into a small basket for her.

Aaron set the basket of eggs on the table, pulled out a chair, and sat. "You two are to stay close to the house for a while. No wandering off to the creek alone. No trips to the outhouse at night."

"And you are going to tell us why, right?"

"I found some moccasin prints at the back corner of the chicken coop."

"Are we missing chickens?"

By now, Jeremy was standing. He waited for his pa to answer.

"No. No, we're not missing any chickens. Or eggs. Whoever was out there is not interested in the chickens. They've been watching the house."

"I see."

Sarah looked at Jeremy. He was agitated. He kept rubbing his hands together. "It's all right, Jeremy. Nothing to worry about." She smoothed a lock of hair from his forehead. "Just someone passing through, I'm sure."

The boy walked to his pa's side. He extended a timid hand and stroked Aaron's throat.

Sarah shivered. Her eyes met Aaron's. "Did you..."

"No. I did not."

Jeremy hugged his pa, then turned and walked out the door. Aaron and Sarah watched as he sat down under his favorite tree. After a few moments, he was joined by a squirrel.

Jeremy had seen the rope. One of the men had it draped over his saddle horn the day they took his pa away. Pa had told him to hide in the root cellar while he talked to the men. When Aaron opened the door, Jeremy saw the rope. Once his pa was outside, he snuck out the back door quietly and ran to the cellar, where he waited, and worried, and finally fell asleep. Jeremy remembered the day very clearly. That was the day Sarah came to them. He'd known that she would come. He just hadn't known when. Several months after "the day," which is what he called the day his mother disappeared, the a-ha-wi had come to him. He'd been down at the creek, catching crawdads. He'd looked up to see the huge animal standing on the opposite bank, watching him. The animal had not moved, but Jeremy had heard the voice from inside the beast. The one that spoke to his own inner voice.

The stag had told him there would soon be a woman. A woman who was different from his mama but would eventually love him as his mama had done. That this woman would love him, and his papa, and that she would one day kill to protect him. He had seen the "leg gun" that Sarah wore. He never doubted she was brave. As he slept in the cellar, the day before she had come, he had dreamed of Sarah killing a man to protect his papa, so he knew that when it was time, Sarah would keep him safe.

Chapter Seven

Aaron leaned against the porch post and stared at the rain as he sipped his coffee. It was the wettest fall Aaron could remember. He imagined the folks on down the creek from him were doing a lot of wading. He was glad Granny was as far back from Paint Creek as he was. It was already a good three feet out of its banks.

He'd had to string a clothesline across the dining room for Sarah, a few days ago.

She'd been fussing about not having her electric dryer, whatever that was, but at least she'd laughed when she got up the next morning and found the line.

Maybe he and Jeremy had better go check on Granny this morning, just to make sure the old girl was all right.

The screen door squeaked open, and he turned to see Sarah step out.

"Mind some company?"

He smiled. "Nope, drag up a chair, and count the drops with me."

Sara laughed. "Well at least it's letting up enough to count them."

"I was just thinking I'd take Jeremy and go down to check on Granny, make sure she's all right. She likes to think she can do anything, but she has to be close to ninety-one or two. This weather causes my bones to ache some. I hate to think of how she might be feeling."

"That's probably a good idea. I just put a cake in the oven, so you boys will have to go without me."

"Sarah, stay in the house while we're gone. I don't want you out wandering around. I haven't seen any tracks lately, but the rain would have washed them away."

"I'm not feeling the urge to do any mudding today."

"Any what?" Aaron raised an eyebrow.

"It's what they call it when they take their trucks…oh, never mind. Let's just say I won't be out rolling in the mud like a pig, okay?"

Aaron shook his head. Sometimes he wished he understood what the heck she was talking about.

A half hour later, the rain had stopped, and Sarah watched as they rode away.

She walked back into the cabin and surveyed her little world. She had a good fire going in the fireplace. The boys would be gone at least three hours. If she hurried and finished the laundry, she should be able to squeeze in a hot bath before they got home.

****

Aaron was glad to see the creek had not breached the road between his place and Granny's. He'd be willing to bet that pond behind her house had overflowed its berm, though. Well, from its position on the property, it would run away from the cabin. The old man had been a pretty good engineer.

Aaron turned to look at Jeremy. The boy had on Aaron's old slicker, and it covered him from head to toe and then some. Aaron smiled. He could remember when he was that age and couldn't wait to wear his pa's things, to feel older, to make believe he was grown.

The smile faded slowly. Jeremy had grown up way too fast. He'd left his smiling, laughing childhood behind the day his ma disappeared.

Well, the boy loved Granny, so this visit was a good thing.

They were not met by ol' Red's baying. Not a good sign.

Aaron stopped the horses. He slid off his mount, and motioned for Jeremy to do the same.

"Son, stand here, behind your horse, while I see if Granny is home."

Jeremy nodded and took his pa's reins. He peered around his horse as Aaron stepped quietly toward the cabin, looking all around as he moved.

When Aaron was close to the cabin, he called out, "Granny, you in there?"

Then Red began howling from inside.

Aaron motioned for Jeremy to stay where he was. He was about to yell again when the door opened slowly.

"Well, don't you chickens have sense enough to get in out of the rain?"

Aaron burst out laughing and turned to wave to Jeremy to come on up. By the time they had hung their slickers by the door, Granny had a kettle on.

"What are you doin' out in this mess, anyway?" she asked.

"I just wanted to make sure all the rain hadn't washed you away."

"Pshaw! It'd take more than a good rain to wash me away."

When she turned from the stove, Aaron could see she was limping.

"Granny, what have you done? What's wrong with that left foot?"

"Well, not anything you're gonna be able to fix. I'm gettin' old. That's what's wrong with it. I sorta slipped in the mud yesterday, when I was feedin' the chickens. It was swelled up this mornin', so the poor things ain't been fed yet."

Before Aaron could respond, Jeremy walked over and laid a hand on Granny's arm.

"Why, thank you, darlin'. Granny would appreciate that. Just be careful of that ol' dominicker hen. She gets a little testy when you try to sneak the eggs out."

Aaron stood in silence as the boy put on his slicker, picked up a basket from the pantry, and walked out the door.

He turned to Granny. She was smiling at him.

"Me and the boy have an understandin'. He talks on a level I can hear."

Aaron shook his head as he said, "I'm not even going to ask you to explain that."

Granny just cackled, like one of her hens. "Sometimes the very old and the very young have more betwixt them than you-uns in the middle."

When Jeremy returned a short while later, the basket was full of eggs, and his reward was a piece of pie.

"Granny, I want you to stay off that foot. I'll ride back down tomorrow and check on you. It'll be a couple of days before all the mud dries up, and I don't want to ride up here and find you lying in the yard 'cause you couldn't make it to the house."

Granny looked at him for several minutes.

Aaron could tell she was fixing to have something

to say about that.

She finally nodded, but what she said was, "Why don't you leave Jeremy with me for a couple of days? Me and him and Red could have us a good visit. He can take care of the chickens and such. That'd save you runnin' up and down the road." Then she added, "Besides, you got enough to take care of at your place, right?" The grin Granny flashed told Aaron she wasn't talking about the farm animals.

Aaron could feel his face starting to heat up, but Jeremy walked around the table, laid his hand on his arm, and nodded his head at him.

"Well. I guess you two think you've put one over on me, don't you? All right, if that's how it's gonna be, then I'll be heading back to the house. Jeremy, you take good care of Granny, and mind what she says."

The two of them walked him to the door.

Aaron stepped outside to find only his horse tied to the rail. He turned back to find Jeremy looking innocent and Granny grinning like a possum. The boy had already stabled his horse.

"All right, you two, behave, and I'll see you in two days."

****

Sarah was wakened by the sound of boots on the porch. Good grief, she had fallen asleep in the tub. She sat up and frantically grabbed for the blanket, warming on a chair by the fire. The door opened just as her hand found it. She stood, turned, and covered herself in one smooth motion. At least she thought it was smooth. A half second later, she knew she had overcompensated and was slowly tilting over.

Aaron took in the scene with one glance. He could

tell by the look of panic on her face that she was falling. Two long strides and one short lunge later, he had both arms around her. Her back was wet, and his hands slid over her ribs.

Sarah closed her eyes and held her breath as his hands pressed her closer to his chest. They were frozen in place, with neither wanting to move.

"I think I'm okay now. If you want to let go, I'll just step out of the tub." Sarah was breathless.

Aaron finally looked down at her. Her face was upturned, and her mouth was slightly open. He slowly ran one hand down her wet back.

Her eyes widened. "Where is Jeremy?"

Without breaking eye contact and still rubbing her back, Aaron began to lower his mouth to hers as he murmured, "He's staying the night with Granny."

Sarah had no time for a response, as his mouth took ownership of hers.

The kiss started slow and sweet. And then the fire overtook them both.

"Sarah," Aaron whispered. "Sarah, you have to tell me you want this."

She raised her head to meet his gaze, then slowly released the blanket, allowing it to puddle on the floor between them.

Aaron scooped her up and headed to his bedroom.

Those few steps gave Sarah a moment for rational thought. There would be no turning back from this. Once she gave in to him, she would be vulnerable. Was she ready to give her whole heart again? Could she say no to the fire his mouth had started?

Aaron stopped by the bed and set her on her feet. He looked down, and she was swaying, her eyes closed.

His hand cupped one breast. Sarah's eyes flew open, her mind shocked by the intensity of the feeling, then closed again as she gave way to the heat building inside her.

"Last chance, Sarah," he whispered raggedly, as if the very act of breathing was difficult.

Opening her eyes, she began to unbutton his shirt.

****

Sarah was dreaming. She was walking in the forest. She was lost, and every tree seemed to create a slithering shadow on the ground. She wanted to call out for help, but a voice inside her said no, no, don't let them know where you are. There was a crashing sound behind her, and she began to run. She looked down and found she was holding Jeremy's hand. They were running together. Running from what? There was a deep rumbling, and another crashing sound, and Sarah woke with a scream.

She was fighting the bedcovers, thrashing from side to side.

"Sarah! Sarah, wake up!"

Aaron finally had to encircle her in his arms, bedcovers and all, to still her thrashing. She was panting as if she had just run a mile.

"Sarah, look at me. Open your eyes. That's right, look at me. There you are. Honey, it was a dream. You were just dreaming."

Sarah drew in a long, ragged breath, then exhaled slowly.

"I'm sorry. I was lost in the woods, and then there was this crashing sound…"

Even as she spoke, the lightning cracked outside, lighting the entire room for a flash of a second. The resulting thunder was immediate and deafening.

Aaron tightened his hold on her as she cringed.

"That's the crashing sound you heard, sweetheart, just thunder and lightning, that's all. It's been going on for a while now."

"I'm sorry. I didn't mean to wake you." Sarah was suddenly very aware that she was naked and in Aaron's bed. She relaxed enough for him to let go of her, and then she turned her back and slid to the edge of the bed.

"Sarah, it's early. Lie back down and—"

"No," she interrupted him. "No, I...I have to use the night bucket. In my room." And with that declaration, she practically ran from the room.

Aaron lay back in the bed and waited. And waited. When it was finally evident that she was not returning, he rolled to his side and slept.

Sarah was wide awake. The dream had jerked her from a deep slumber, but it was the awareness of what she had done that kept her from returning to sleep. She couldn't blame Aaron. She was a grown woman, and she had wanted it as much as he did. Maybe more. Now she wasn't so sure.

Her heart told her she could not live under his roof, with his son, without this relationship having the blessing of the Lord. It wasn't right, and Sarah had been raised to do the right thing, but she would not force him. He had to want to share his life with her. She had to know that he wanted her. For all time.

And so she stayed in her bed, in her room, alone, and waited for sunrise.

Chapter Eight

Aaron woke with a start. He looked around the room quickly. Everything looked normal. Then his gaze moved to the right side of the bed. He let out a long sigh as he remembered. He had made love to Sarah.

He had wanted to be gentle and slow, but her response to his body had spurred them both to pure heat. Several times. Then she had left the bed and not returned.

He didn't think he had hurt her. Maybe he should check on her.

Aaron dressed quietly and moved to the kitchen. He stoked the fire in the stove and put on the coffee. Then he walked softly to Sarah's door. He listened but could hear nothing.

He slowly eased the door open. Rays from the early morning sun turned her bare shoulders to gold. Her hair was splayed across the pillow, and he wanted nothing more than to climb in there beside her and hold her while she slept. But she had left his bed of her own accord. He closed the door gently. He would just have to wait for her to explain.

****

The sun slowly pushed the sleep from Sarah's eyes. She stretched her long legs toward the end of the bed, and a muscle in her thigh tightened. She immediately stopped moving, and her eyes flew open. Remembrance washed over her. The tightness in her thighs was from the several times Aaron had made love to her. No, not *to* her but *with* her. They had made sweet, passionate love. Three times, if her memory served.

Sarah looked at the window. Good heavens, it must be near noontime. She had slept the morning away. Her mind was running in circles while she dressed. What should she say to Aaron? How to tell him that this would not happen again unless they were married? Did that sound like an ultimatum? That was not what she wanted.

Finally dressed, Sarah sat on the edge of the bed and tried to calm herself. She closed her eyes and took long, slow breaths. And then she prayed.

Lord, I've never claimed to be a perfect person, but I've always tried to live a good life, no matter how often I've failed. Lord, I need strength and guidance. Surely there is some reason I woke up in this place and time. Help me to see the reason and understand the purpose. Amen.

She opened the door and stepped into the kitchen. Aaron must have been up a good while. The tub was gone, along with the blanket she had dropped on the floor. Her face flamed at the thought of the invitation she had given him.

Sarah was lost in remembering when the front door opened. She welcomed the cooling air that rushed in.

Aaron stopped short. Lord, she was beautiful, standing there looking unsure and almost timid.

"Good morning, sleepyhead. I held off on breakfast so you could have it fresh when you woke." He carried the basket of eggs to the table, slowly removed his coat and hung it over the chair, then turned to face Sarah.

She was staring at the floor.

He walked over and took her in his arms. She did not resist.

"Sarah, we need to talk. You don't just share what we shared last night and then go about your business as if nothing has changed."

She stepped out of his arms and walked halfway round the table before she pulled out a chair and dropped into it.

"You're right, of course. We must talk."

Sarah watched as he poured two cups of coffee, placed one in front of her, and walked to the other side of the table with his.

Once he was seated, he took a sip, then met her gaze.

"All right, Sarah, tell me what's on your mind."

"I…I want you to know that I'm not in the habit of…you are the first man…" Her voice trailed off. She could not look at him.

"Sarah. Sarah, please look at me."

Sarah finally raised her head and met his gaze.

"Sarah, I haven't been with a lot of women in my life, but I know the difference between a loose woman and a good one. I know that what happened between us last night was not to be taken lightly. You are the kind of woman who expects commitment and does not give herself lightly. And I'm fine with that, Sarah. In fact, I'm more than fine. I'm darn proud that you considered me a good enough man to give yourself to. And if you'll have me, I think we can build a good life together."

Sarah could see the sincerity in his eyes. He was not just paying her lip service, but there was no mention of love. And what did that mean? *A good life together.* She'd had a good life alone. And, for Sarah, the only thing worse than being alone was being with someone and still feeling alone. She needed more time.

"Could we just pretend, for a few hours, that there is no tomorrow? That we won't have to answer to anyone for our actions, and that we actually love each other?"

Her words were like a knife in his heart. If she needed to pretend that she loved him, then he had lost. But if that was all he could have, then he would take that, for now.

"All right, Sarah. We've got until Jeremy comes home. We can pretend all you want until then." He thought for a moment. "So what would you like to do today? Is there something you think you would enjoy, that we haven't done?" Aaron was going to do everything he could to make the time they had memorable.

Sarah sipped her coffee. If today was all she had, she wanted to make the most of it. If he was not going to love her forever, then he was going to remember her.

"I want you to draw me. I want a drawing that you created."

"A drawing, you say? You want a drawing? Well, I can do that, but I get to choose how I draw you." He smiled like a man who had just won a great prize. "We're almost out of bread, so I want to draw you making bread."

"Oh." Sarah had imagined herself sitting in the sun or reading a book. She thought it odd, but it was his drawing. "Okay. I'll make bread."

She turned to gather the ingredients, but he caught

her arm. She looked up at him questioningly.

He smiled down at her like a fox eyeing a chicken that had strayed from the pen. He had the large apron hung over his arm. He turned her around to face him, and then slowly started unbuttoning her dress.

"What are you doing?" Her voice had dropped to a whisper.

"Why, I'm getting you dressed for your portrait." He slipped the dress off her shoulders, and they were both fascinated by the sight of it sliding down her frame to lie in folds at her feet. He was pleased to see that she wore nothing under the garment.

Sarah should protest. It was the decent thing to do. When she raised her face to voice her misgivings, she was rendered speechless by the look of hunger in his eyes. She knew she would give in to him again, because she was hungry, as well.

She was totally surprised when he hung the apron over her head, turned her around, and began to tie the strings at her back. She turned, only to see him go to the chest of drawers and start removing his drawing papers.

He turned to look at her. "Well, don't just stand there. Make bread."

"You want me to make bread, wearing nothing but an apron?"

"Oh, yes."

His grin reminded Sarah of a teenager with his first girly magazine.

And so she made bread. And every time she had to turn her backside toward him, she wished the apron was larger. And when she had to lean over the table to knead the bread, she was keenly aware of how her bare breasts peeked out of the apron bib. She was also aware that the stick of charcoal in his hand had never stopped moving. He was completely engrossed in his drawing. And somehow, this took away her nervousness. By the time she was ready to put the loaves in the oven, she had forgotten her nakedness.

Aaron had not. He paused to admire his work. He had captured her innocence and her purity, but also her womanly spirit. She was Eve, offering the apple to Adam. She was the dancing Salome. And he wanted her.

Sarah turned from the oven. She caught sight of Aaron's face as he admired his drawing. Sarah had never been a vain woman. She considered herself to be very average. She had seen his talent and suspected it would be a good likeness, but it was the look on Aaron's face as he continued to stare at it that made her want to see it.

She slowly crossed the room and stood beside his chair. "May I see it?"

Aaron looked up at her, and she could see that he was pleased with it. He slowly turned it around toward her.

She was stunned. It was her, but it was not the woman who looked back at her from the mirror in the mornings. The woman in this drawing was not afraid of tomorrow. She lived only for today, for the here and now.

Sarah could feel her body responding to the drawing. She could feel life moving through her veins with every heartbeat.

She laid the drawing down on the table, then very slowly straddled Aaron and lowered herself onto his lap. She took his face in her hands and kissed him as if she was starving and he might be her last meal.

Aaron held himself in check until Sarah began to moan. Then he stood and carried her to the bed.

****

Sarah must have dozed off, because she suddenly woke to the smell of bread.

"Oh, darn," she mumbled under her breath as she tried to untangle herself from Aaron's long legs.

"What is it?"

"The bread. It's going to burn."

He laughed as he drew her back against his side. "I took the bread out of the oven an hour ago. Lie back down and rest."

When she woke again, the windows were dark and the room was filled with lamplight. She raised herself on her elbows to look for Aaron. She found him sitting naked in a chair, his sketchbook on his knee and the floor around him scattered with sketches.

"Hello," he said softly.

"How long did I sleep?"

"About three hours. I'm not sure. I was busy."

She looked at the floor. There must have been at least six drawings at his feet.

"I didn't sleep much last night, so I guess I was catching up."

"I was about to wake you anyway. Come on. I have something for you."

He took both her hands in his and pulled her from the bed. They moved into the dining room, and she stopped abruptly. The table was set, with candles. There was sliced ham, and fresh bread, and a jar of Granny's pickles. However, it was the tub of steaming water in front of the roaring fire that drew her attention.

Sarah's eyes filled with tears. If only this was real. If only they were not pretending. She shut her eyes tightly. She would not cry. She would be the woman in the drawing. She would experience every moment of the next few hours, and she would hold the memory of them in her heart forever.

Chapter Nine

They were having what Granny called a late taste of summer. There'd been no frost yet, and it was nearly the third week of November.

Sarah stepped out on the front porch, coffee in hand. It was early, and the mist was hanging over the top of Viking Mountain. She sipped from her tin cup, then almost broke out laughing.

She had left behind a world that would never know the peace of a quiet cup of coffee with no phones ringing and no television scaring you with the horrors of the day. It was sad, really, she thought. All those modern conveniences just got between people and nature. They kept you from enjoying the things the Lord put here for just that purpose.

Well, she had work to do.

She drained the cup and called out, "Jeremy, I'm going to the washhouse to do some laundry. If you need anything, that's where I'll be."

Aaron had gone hunting this morning, and if she got the lead out, she could get a couple of loads on the line before he got back. She picked up the laundry basket and headed to the washhouse.

Sarah was lost in thought or she might have seen the man standing at the corner of the henhouse. She fired up the potbelly stove, then picked up the bucket to get some water from the well. As she rounded the corner of the washhouse, the man stepped in front of her. He was big. Tall, with dark hair and copper skin. Sarah's breath froze in her lungs, and her heart skipped a beat, but she didn't scream, not until she caught sight of the other man heading for the cabin. As she expelled the breath she'd been holding, she swung the bucket with every bit of force she could muster and screamed at the top of her lungs.

"Jeremy! Run!"

The man had time to take a step back before the bucket slammed into his face. That one step probably saved him from a broken nose, but it did not save his two front teeth. He was spitting blood as he turned to run her down.

Sarah managed only a few yards before he tackled her. She fell face down, with the full weight of the man on top of her. All her breath was knocked out of her, and before she could draw another, he had flipped her over and clipped her chin with a fist that had seen many bar fights. She didn't even have time to think about Jeremy before she lost consciousness.

****

Aaron looked up as a cloud passed over him. Where in the heck had that come from? The sky had been blue and clear a little while ago. If he picked up the pace, he could make it home before the storm. He'd taken longer than he intended. It had been such a peaceful morning. He'd had time to decide what he was going to do about Sarah.

It had been three weeks now since they had made love. She had been sweet but quiet ever since. Of course, it was almost impossible to speak with her privately, now. For some reason, Jeremy had been like her shadow ever since he'd spent the two nights with Granny. It was as if he sensed something was different and he needed to protect her.

Aaron chuckled to himself as he trudged along. He was the last person Jeremy needed to worry about. He had accepted the fact that he loved her and was going to marry her. Now, all he had to do was convince her.

When Aaron broke through the tree line, the first thing he noticed was the door to the washhouse standing open. He was surprised there were no clothes hanging on the line. He looked at the sky again, and now that he was out of the trees, he could see the wall of black clouds moving in quickly out of the southeast. Maybe Sarah had seen them and decided to wait until tomorrow to do laundry. As he got closer to the washhouse, he saw that the door was standing open on the potbelly stove. He dropped the rabbits he'd been carrying and stepped inside to close it. Leaving it open was a good way for a spark to set fire to something.

Halfway to the cabin, he found the bucket. It had a large dent in one side. Aaron bent down and picked it up. The dent had dried blood on it. Aaron's chest began to tighten. He yelled as he ran.

"Sarah? Jeremy?"

By the time he got to the front porch, he was shaking. The door was standing open, and he could see the overturned kitchen chairs.

"Sarah! Jeremy!" Aaron was shouting like a mad man now as he ran out the back door and up the hill to the root cellar.

Aaron jerked open the door. The root cellar was empty. And so were his lungs. The tightness in his chest worsened, and he thought he might vomit. He stood in the doorway, his mind totally blank.

"Horses, man. Yes, they rode to Granny's." Even as he ran to the barn, he kept telling himself that fairytale. He had to believe it. Or go crazy.

Aaron gave no notice to the large raindrops that had started to fall.

He found all three horse stalls empty, and he froze in fear for several moments. He finally ran back to the cabin. He grabbed his .45 and a box of shells from atop the rafters in his bedroom, slung the rifle over his shoulder, and started running.

If the rain had not been coming down in buckets, he might have been able to see where the horses had left the road before they got to Granny's. He might have had an idea where they were headed. However, since they were no longer following an actual trail, any sign of their passing was soon washed away.

****

"Son, you just might as well try to eat something. There ain't a thing you can do in this rain but get wet." Granny was really worried about Aaron. He couldn't take much more.

He'd looked like a wild man when he raced up to her door. And when she told him she hadn't seen the woman or the boy, he had just plain collapsed.

"Well if'n you ain't goin' to eat, the least you can do is get out of those wet clothes. I laid out a set of dry ones on the bed. Hollis would be happy to know you was a-wearin' his things. You know he was always fond of you, son." When Aaron didn't respond, Granny took things into her own hands. "Here, drink this down. Now, doggone it," she snapped.

Aaron looked up to see her holding a cup. He took

the cup and downed the contents in one big gulp. He lost his breath, then began to sputter and cough. It was pure 'shine, and he'd thought it was water.

Granny gave him a couple of minutes to get his breath back. "Now, get yourself in that bedroom, and get outta those wet clothes."

Aaron decided it was easier to just do what she said, so he did.

Granny was waiting for him when he came out.

"Now, that has ta feel better. All right, boy, you have ta listen to me. It is dark as the inside of a coal mine out there, and it's been pourin' down now for at least five hours. Not even Herman Young's old blue-tick hound could find a scent in all that mud. You're just gonna have to wait until the rain slows some afore you take off lookin' for them two. That girl struck me as bein' pretty levelheaded, and we know Jeremy has weathered tough things afore, so they's gonna be all right. You'll see."

However, when Granny sat down and opened her worn Bible, Aaron had to turn away so she wouldn't see his tears.

****

Sarah was wet to the bone when she regained consciousness. She was tied to Aaron's mare in such a manner that she could not see behind her. Her body felt like it had been riding for hours. She prayed that Jeremy had escaped and hidden in the root cellar, but she had her doubts. The big man who had knocked her out was leading her horse. They were moving through dense trees, at a slight incline. It was so dark that Sarah could barely see the man's back.

She was wondering if they were lost when the

animals suddenly stopped. The big man slid off his horse and disappeared into the wall of rain. She imagined she saw a spark and then a faint light. The blackness was so thick that when the man suddenly appeared at her side, she yelped, causing her horse to prance around. The big man grabbed the reins and growled at her. There was a sharp tug, and suddenly the ropes that had been holding her on the horse fell away. She swayed for a moment, then flinched when the man grabbed her around the waist and jerked her off the horse. Her legs would not hold her, and she found herself face down in the mud. He jerked her up by one arm and directed her toward the faint light.

Sarah found herself in a large cave. She had been able to walk right through the opening, while her captor had to bend over to keep from knocking himself out. Once inside, he was able to stand. She heard a scuffle behind her, and she turned to see another man shove Jeremy through the opening. The boy stumbled but managed to stay upright.

Once he got his balance, he raised his head, and the first thing he saw was Sarah. While he did not smile, she could see the relief in his eyes. He ran straight to her and buried his face in her side. Though her hands were still tied, she was able to hold him close to her body. She could feel him trembling—whether from fear or the cold rain, it didn't matter. They were together.

"Git yerselves back against that far wall and sit down. And don't even think about givin' me any grief, 'cause I'm tired, cold, and damned near drowned because of you-uns."

This was the man Sarah had seen go into the cabin where Jeremy had been.

She guided Jeremy back toward the wall, and they both sat on the rock floor, as close together as possible. Sarah began to look around. There was what looked like at least half a cord of wood piled against the opposite wall. To the left of that was another opening, possibly leading to another room in the cave, but the lantern was not bright enough to pierce that darkness. The woodpile indicated this was not a random choice of hiding place. This had been a pre-meditated action on the part of these two.

The men were standing at the front entrance, staring off into the darkness, as if waiting for something—or someone.

"You kin be damn sure he ain't comin' out in this rain tonight. Oh, no, he's holed up somewheres, dry and warm, 'cause he's got us to do his dirty work." The shorter man turned from the opening and moved to the woodpile. "Well, light or no light, I'm startin' a fire. I don't aim to freeze to death. Hell, ain't nobody gonna be out in this storm that even knows this place is here." And with that, he started placing some rocks in a circle and laying the firewood inside the ring. Within minutes he had a good fire going, and while it lit the inside of the cave well, it would be a while before any of them felt any change in the near-freezing temperature.

Sarah had been watching the short man build the fire and did not realize the big one had left until he walked back through the opening, carrying saddle blankets. He must have unsaddled the horses and secured them somewhere.

When he started toward her, she had to force herself to meet his stare. She didn't want to appear belligerent. She understood they were in danger. She was eternally grateful that she had put on her jeans this morning. Neither of the men had seen her gun, and she wanted to keep it that way until the moment she had to use it.

The big guy stopped directly in front of her. She met his gaze without flinching. She could see his lip was cut and swollen. She wondered what her face must look like. She held up her tied hands toward the man. After a long moment, he took a bowie knife from the scabbard on his belt and, with one long swipe, cut the ropes. He then threw one of the blankets at her. There were actually some dry spots on it. She tugged Jeremy right in under her arm and arranged the blanket around them both. When she looked back up, the man was still looking at her. She thought a moment, then slowly nodded her thanks. He finally turned away.

"Myers, you get first watch. I'm goin' to sleep." And with that, the big man curled up under the other blanket and within minutes was snoring loudly.

Myers grumbled under his breath for a while. Then he too made himself comfortable near the fire.

When she thought Myers was asleep, Sarah tapped Jeremy on the arm. He immediately raised his eyes to her, which told her he had not been dozing, as she had first thought.

"Are you okay, sweetie?"

Jeremy nodded slowly, then reached up to touch her face.

Yep, just as she thought, it must look pretty bad.

"Don't worry, honey. I'm all right, just a little cold. Was I out for a long time?"

He nodded yes.

"Were you able to see where we are? Could you

find your way back home?"

Jeremy held out one hand, and with the other he made the motion of walking across his exposed palm.

Sarah thought about that for a minute. "Do you mean we crossed something? Like a bridge?"

Jeremy nodded no, then wiggled his fingers like running water.

"You mean we're on the other side of Paint Creek?"

He nodded yes. Then he spread his arms out wide, with his fingers waving.

It took a few minutes for her to catch on. "Oh, you mean the creek was big?"

He nodded yes, then gestured that the falling rain had made the creek big. He couldn't think of a way to tell her how the horses had struggled to get through the deep, swiftly moving water. Or that one of the men had said if it kept up like this, there would be a bad flood in the bottomland.

"Well," Sarah whispered softly, "after all the rain we've had, and as hard as it's coming down now, I wouldn't be surprised if half the mountain didn't slide down. We can't think about doing anything in this darkness, so we may as well try to sleep. Just lay your head in my lap."

Jeremy took Sarah's hand in his smaller one, adjusted his body sideways, and curled up in her lap. His complete trust in her was so innocent. While it warmed her heart, her eyes began to fill with tears. She dashed them away with the back of one cold hand. She didn't have time for that now. She had to plan. She had four bullets and would have to make the most of them.

****

Aaron woke with a start and a shout. He looked around wildly, saw he was at Granny's, then slumped back against the sofa. He looked at the window above the sink. It was dark. Not the dark before daybreak but the dark of a heavy rain, which was confirmed by the roar on the tin roof.

He wiped a trembling hand across his face. Lord, it had been the longest night he'd ever spent, and he still didn't know what to do. He did know he could not sit here doing nothing or he'd go crazy. Aaron stood and immediately had to hold onto a chair. He hadn't eaten since night before last.

Granny walked out of her bedroom just in time to see Aaron swaying as he held on to one of her ladderback chairs.

"Just set your behind right down in that chair you're a-hangin' onto. You gotta eat somethin' before you take out of here. No, don't give me that look. I know you. Even though there's not a single thing you can do, I know full well that ain't gonna stop ya from runnin' on out there. Why don't you go saddle up my old mare, and by the time you do that I'll have some hot food ready for ya."

Aaron stopped and kissed Granny on her gray head as he headed for the door.

She'd just finished reheating last night's offerings when Aaron returned dripping water everywhere.

He sat looking at the plate Granny had filled with bacon, some greens, and cornbread. He knew she would be hurt if he didn't at least try, so he lifted a forkful to his mouth. It was all sawdust to him.

Granny sat across from him and sipped on her coffee. "Have ya come up with some sort of plan?"

Aaron laid the fork down. "I guess I'll just try riding the creek in both directions, in case they get away and try to make it back home." It sounded even more lame when he said it out loud.

Granny could hear the despair in his voice.

"All right, son, that ain't a bad idea. And if'n you meet anyone along the road, maybe they mighta seen somethin' that might help."

****

Sarah woke with a start and jerked her head upward, slamming the back of it against the rock wall. Her whole body jumped from the impact, waking Jeremy from a deep sleep.

He raised his face to her and waited patiently.

"Sorry," she said softly. "I must have been dreaming, and I knocked my head on the wall. I didn't mean to wake you."

He just nodded.

Sarah watched as Myers put more wood on the fire, but the big guy was nowhere to be seen. She thought she'd been pretty darn patient, but she was tired, hungry, and her face still hurt. She wanted some answers.

"Just how long do you think you're gonna keep us here?" she snapped.

Myers jumped at the sudden sound of her voice, dropping the log he'd been holding. Sparks and cinders flew as the log crashed onto the fire.

The man seemed embarrassed at being startled.

"Don't start gettin' smart with me, bitch. We'll keep ya as long as we damn well feel like it," he shouted. He was walking toward her as he spoke, and stopped a foot or so in front of her. He stood scowling down at her.

He was not a big man, but Sarah wasn't sure if she could take him physically. She couldn't very well shoot him while the big guy was outside. He'd hear the shot and be warned. She'd just have to wait.

"I need to go to the bathroom." She raised her chin defiantly.

"Well, look around. Do ya see an outhouse? Just go where ya are," Myers growled.

Before she could reply, the other man returned. He stopped just inside the doorway and took in the scene with one look.

"Myers, skin these rabbits, and I'll make some stew." He extended his left hand, and Sarah could see he held three rabbits.

"I ain't yer damn cook," Myers shouted. At least he had turned his back on Sarah and was now shouting at the big guy.

"You were too lazy to get up and go find breakfast, so now you can skin it." The man had at least three inches on Myers, and a good fifty pounds.

Myers just grunted as he jerked the rabbits out of the other man's extended hand.

Sarah looked up at the big man. "Do you have a name?"

He stared back at her for several heartbeats before answering. "Cooper. Just Cooper."

"Well, Mr. Cooper, we need to relieve ourselves, and I'm not doing it here."

"Lady, I seen you run, so you ain't doing it outside, either." He picked up a lantern and approached her. "You can go in there, but watch for snakes." He jerked his head toward the black hole in the far wall.

The whole idea of meeting a snake in there did not sit well with Sarah, but it was probably the best offer she was going to get from these two.

She stood slowly, leaning against the wall. Her rib cage was very sore, whether it was from the tackle when she ran or from being tied to the horse, one or the other had left its mark. She slowly took the lantern, being careful not to stretch too far.

"Thank you." She looked down at Jeremy. "You can go when I get back."

She raised the lantern high as she entered the second room. She looked all around the small alcove, praying to find another way out. Nothing, just solid rock. On closer inspection, she found the rock was not as solid as it first looked. A large crack had formed in the farthest wall, and water was seeping in at a pretty good pace. A good-sized puddle had formed on the floor of the room. She wondered just how much wet mountainside was pushing against that wall— mountainside that now had several days of water weight added to it.

****

There was no way to tell how much time had passed, but Sarah figured it was early afternoon. The darkness inside the cave had not changed with the passage of time. The stew had been a little bland, but it had been hot, with plenty of meat. Both the men were now stretched out near the fire, patiently waiting for something or someone. While they had been speaking quietly, she was sure one of them had used the name Taggart. She and Jeremy had to get out before Taggart arrived.

Cooper was still wearing his gunbelt, but Myers

had removed his while skinning the rabbits. She could see it lying on top of the woodpile. All right, then, Cooper would get the first bullet.

She and Jeremy sat with their backs to the wall, their knees raised. Sarah slowly pulled the blanket up to cover their legs.

Cooper gave them a quick glance. He got up and strolled to the pile, picked up a couple of pieces of wood, and walked back toward the fire.

By now, Sarah had her pistol in her hand, under the blanket. She waited until he placed the wood on the fire. Then she stood. She was turned sideways, with her gun hand toward Jeremy.

Cooper looked toward her.

"Did you need something?"

Sarah turned and fired, in one smooth motion.

Cooper took the bullet in the upper thigh, just as she had intended. She was not going to have another dead man on her conscience. As Cooper was sinking to the floor, Myers was frantically scrambling to get to his gun. His bullet hit the back of his right thigh. While Cooper had grunted when hit, Myers screamed like a banshee.

Jeremy was now on his feet and moving toward the front opening.

Keeping her eye on Myers, she yelled at Cooper, "Unfasten that gun belt real slow, and don't do anything stupid. You had a partner named Ryker that never made it home, right? Well, I'm not proud of it, but he's dead. You might have a limp, but at least you'll be alive. That's right, now just toss it toward the boy."

Cooper thought about it for a couple of heartbeats, then tossed the belt.

Sarah made a wide circle and retrieved Myers' gun. The man was still writhing and screaming. She met Jeremy by the cave opening. A quick look told her the darkness was from the pouring rain, and that it would only get darker as the afternoon faded.

Both men had placed their hats on an outcropping of rock to dry. Sarah took one and handed the other to Jeremy. When he looked at her questioningly, she said, "To keep the water out of our eyes."

She turned back to the men. Cooper was slowly tying his neckerchief around his upper leg, trying to stanch the blood flow. Poor Myers was openly crying as he cursed her.

"Where are the horses?"

Myers couldn't hear her over his own screaming. Cooper slowly shook his head no.

So be it, she thought. He figured that if she hadn't already killed them, she wasn't going to, so he wasn't going to tell her a damn thing.

She shoved his hat down on her head and ran out.

****

Aaron had stopped feeling the rain several hours ago. It was getting nigh onto four in the afternoon, he figured. Darkness would roll in quickly, given all the rain clouds. Granny had been right. With this downpour, there was no way a tracker could read sign or a dog could find a scent, no matter how good either were.

Paint Creek was now a roaring river. He'd already seen bushes and small trees breaking loose from the banks. The flow was strong, approaching dangerous. He just prayed to the Lord that Sarah and Jeremy were on the east side. He was afraid Granny's old mare couldn't make it across or he would have already crossed over to search the west bank first. That side was dotted with old caves that could collapse under the weight of the rain-soaked mountain, and if that happened, the mountain would slide right down into the creek.

Aaron's mind was so full of all the awful things that might have happened to the only family he had left that he was actually sick to his stomach.

It had been a month since he and Sarah had made love. She had been adamant that it would not happen again. He had not pushed her on that, and now he wished he had. He loved her. And she loved him right back. It was just that convincing her had turned out to be a little harder than he'd expected. He had intended to take her into Greeneville when Christmas came, and marry her. Of course, he might have had to hogtie her and drag her there, but he'd been prepared to, if necessary.

Aaron drew in the mare. What was that, maybe a hundred yards ahead? He wiped the rain from his eyes, then snapped the reins. The faithful old mare moved forward. Whatever it was, it was waiting for him, not trying to run. In the darkening gloom, it took Aaron several moments to realize what he was seeing. It was the elusive stag, the stag he often saw in times of distress.

The stag raised his head slowly, as if to say, "It took you long enough." He pawed the muddy ground he stood on, then snorted loudly, his breath creating a large cloud of mist in the cold rain. The old mare was a little nervous and backed away, trembling.

Aaron patted the mare's neck. "I know, girl. He makes me a little skittish too, but just be still for me. I don't think he'll stay long."

The stag lowered his widespread antlers almost to the ground, then raised his head and stared at Aaron.

Aaron's heart was pounding so hard he could hear it echoing in his ears.

At last the huge beast turned and stepped right out into Paint Creek. He appeared to cross the fast-moving water without effort and disappeared up the mountain on the other side.

Aaron sat there, frozen in thought. What did it mean? Why was he seeing the stag now? He turned in the saddle and looked all around him. Nothing. It must mean something. Aaron climbed off the mare and led her the fifty or so yards to a huge sycamore that still had a few leaves. It wasn't much shelter for either of them, but he couldn't convince himself to leave the area after seeing the stag. He would wait until dark before heading back to Granny's.

****

Sarah could not believe it was still raining so hard. She had only just stepped out of the cave and already she was soaked. When she spotted Jeremy, he began to point and wave. Hurray, he had found the horses! They were about twenty yards away, attached to a picket line. He was already sawing on the line with his knife.

When Sarah was about ten feet away, the hair on her arms began to stand. Before she could call out to Jeremy, she was blinded by a flash. She screamed and ducked as splinters of wood flew past her. When her eyes readjusted to the near darkness, she found Jeremy on the ground and the horses were disappearing into the forest.

Dear Lord, don't let him be hurt. Sarah kept

repeating this prayer as she ran to him. Her training kicked in. Find a pulse. *Yes! And his chest is moving. Oh, dear Lord, thank you.*

Jeremy opened his eyes, and as they focused, a look of terror washed over his face. He raised a hand to point over her shoulder.

Sarah ducked, rolled to the right, and was never so glad to still be holding her pistol when she bolted to a standing position. Cooper was as shocked as Sarah when the bullet struck him. His size kept his brain from accepting what his heart already knew. He managed to take several more steps and actually grabbed Sarah's arm before he fell at her feet.

She was still frozen in place when Jeremy threw both arms around her waist. She looked down at his upturned face. The trust reflected in those big eyes took her breath away. And in that moment, she understood that she loved him—and his father—more than she had ever loved anyone in her life. And she would tell Aaron the moment she saw him.

"Come on, sweetie. We've got to get away from here."

Then began two hours of slipping and sliding their way down the thickly treed slope. Every branch and shrub was slick with forest mold, from all the rain. The very air they breathed had that musky, damp overtone.

Sarah had no idea which direction the horses had run, but she figured they would be home before dark. If only she and Jeremy had the same built-in GPS as those horses!

As the trees got thinner, the ground became a little more level. Sarah had hoped to clear the forest before sunset, but with the heavy rains, the level of gray remained the same. She had no idea what time it was, what was east or west, or which way was home. In either case, they had to put distance between themselves and the cave.

Sarah didn't know how long she'd been hearing a low roar before she identified it as moving water, swiftly moving water. She turned to make sure Jeremy was right behind her, and when she turned back she found her path blocked by the largest stag she had ever seen.

She was very proud of the fact that she did not scream. She was not so proud of the fact that she had stopped so abruptly she slipped in the mud and found herself on her backside, practically underneath the huge beast.

The animal never gave her a moment's notice. He only had eyes for Jeremy.

Sarah rose and looked from one to the other. If she'd been asked, she would have sworn they were communicating. She stood very still as Jeremy moved to the animal's side and rested his head against that giant ribcage. After a few moments, Jeremy raised his head, and Sarah was amazed to see a smile on that little face. It was as if all worry had been lifted from his shoulders and all was right with the world.

Sarah made eye contact with the beast, and her heart stopped. It took the space of about three resting beats for her to realize what she should have seen immediately. The painting. This was the grand beast from the painting in the den.

"It is you, isn't it?" Sarah could hear the awe in her own voice, as she spoke.

The stag blinked, then turned and started down the

slope.

Jeremy followed the stag without question. Sarah followed them both, but she was full of questions. Her mind was so full of "What the heck?" and "Are you kidding me?" that she had not been conscious of the growing intensity of the roar until they stepped out of the tree line.

"Oh, my Lord." There was Paint Creek right in front of her, but it was not the Paint Creek she had seen days ago. This was a raging river. It had come out of its banks and was littered with small trees and brush, all of which was sweeping its way downstream at a high rate of speed.

The stag looked up and down the creek, as if searching for something, then finally turned upstream and began to pick its way along the ever-rising waterline.

Sarah and Jeremy followed, as if there was nothing odd about having a huge wild animal for a guide.

"Jeremy," she shouted above the roar, "does any of this look familiar to you?"

The boy never turned, just shook his head from side to side as he kept pace with the stag.

The sun, if it was still up there, gave no light. The many shades of gray had deepened to almost complete darkness when the stag stopped. He raised his majestic head and gave a huge roar.

Sarah was so startled she almost slipped into the rushing water. She scuttled herself back from the edge. Wait—did she see movement on the other side? Was someone there?

"Hello," she shouted. Nothing. "Hello, is someone there?" She screamed so loud the second time she thought she might have damaged her throat.

The shadow moved closer to the opposite bank. "Sarah? Sarah, it's Aaron!"

She burst into tears when she recognized his voice. So much for being a pillar of strength, she thought.

"Sarah, listen to me, honey. The stag will help you across. Can you hold onto him?"

Sarah looked at that forty feet of raging water and was more frightened than she could ever remember being.

"I'll try."

"I'll be right here, sweetheart, just hold onto the stag, okay?"

The stag gave her one long stare, then snorted.

"All right, all right, I'm coming." If she lived through this, she thought, she was gonna have one heck of a story to tell her grandkids.

She put Jeremy in front of her, with his arms around the stag's neck. She grabbed a good handful of the thick winter coat, and they slowly slipped into the freezing water. Sarah didn't panic until they were actually in the stream. It was all she could do to hold onto the beast and keep her head above water. Her left hand had a death grip on the pelt and her right was holding onto Jeremy.

They were about halfway across when it happened. Sarah heard a horrendous cracking sound, followed by a roar. Part of the mountain had given way, and it hit the creek somewhere upstream.

She could feel the stag shudder beneath her hand. Aaron was screaming for her to hurry. She was grateful it was now so dark she could not see what was coming at them. She felt the mighty stag surge forward, and suddenly she could see Aaron. He had a rope tied round his waist, but she couldn't see what was securing the other end. He was leaning out over the water, his arms outstretched.

Suddenly the stag screamed. Something had struck the poor beast, and he was torn from Sarah's grip. She jerked Jeremy to her chest just as the beast was washed downstream. Sara caught a glimpse of a huge log but was too busy trying to stay above the raging water to see more.

She could hear Aaron screaming at her as she fought to hold onto Jeremy. Five more feet. She slipped under the swirling water once, twice, but managed to find the strength to hold Jeremy above the surface. She was finally close enough to shove the boy at his father's outstretched hand. As Sarah went under for the third time, she felt something clawing at her throat, and she thought she heard a high-pitched voice screaming, "Sarah! Sarah!"

Aaron hauled the screaming child from the water and searched frantically for Sarah. Nothing. The darkness of the night settled into his heart as he used the rope to guide himself and Jeremy away from the raging waters. He wouldn't realize until he got back to Granny's that the boy was clutching Sarah's arrowhead necklace as he cried her name over and over again.

Chapter Ten

Greeneville, Tennessee, December 2016

Lisa Kramer called her husband's name a second time.

"Frank, are you even listening?"

Frank Kramer slowly turned to his wife. "Did you say something?"

She shook her head from side to side. "Where on earth were you? I've been telling you for ten minutes that I need you to fetch me the Christmas decorations out of the attic. You don't have to do anything with them, just set all the boxes in the garage. I didn't think you'd want my pregnant self waddling up and down that narrow stairway toting boxes."

"Lord, no! I'll get them for you. Don't even think about trying to climb those stairs. Just sit there and drink your hot chocolate. I'll have them down in no time."

Frank kissed her forehead before heading to the attic stairs. He should be ashamed of himself. He was usually a very thoughtful husband, but his mind had been working overtime lately. He found himself constantly replaying the Sarah Haskins folder in his head. He had reread the original responding officers' notes dozens of times.

It was just that every time he opened that folder,

that face spoke to him. Yesterday it had practically screamed at him. He'd opened the file to read the notes he himself had added.

Yes, he had alerted her bank to notify him of any action on her accounts. He'd found she was actually a rather wealthy young woman. The two life insurance policies from her aunt and uncle had raised her bank account to the healthy side of three hundred thousand. While her prorated payment to the Greene County Electric Co-Op was still being handled with an automatic electronic withdrawal each month, there had been no other activity.

Yes, he had personally spoken to each of her co-workers. He had performed all the standard operating procedures but still had that "something left undone" feeling.

"Enough!" he snapped aloud to himself. "It's almost Christmas. Let it go, for now." He started looking for the boxes marked "X-mas."

Frank had moved four boxes into the garage when Lisa stuck her head out.

"Bless your heart, thank you, sweetie. Just for that, I'm gonna cook your favorite dinner."

Frank smiled at his beautiful wife. "No need to butter me up now. The boxes are down. Were there four or five?"

"You know, I can't remember."

"That's all right. I'll take another look around up there." Frank trudged back up the stairs, noting the beating of his heart in his ears as he neared the top. *That's it, I'm gonna have to lose ten pounds.* His annual physical agility test was in three months, and he wasn't getting any younger.

He stood in the middle of the attic, and eyed the four corners. What was that box behind that old chair? He sat in the chair and pulled the box around to sit between his feet. It wasn't marked and was taped closed. He took out his knife and carefully slit the tape.

Oh. That box. He had started to go through it when they first moved in, but he hadn't made it past the top. After his father's funeral, his mother had insisted he take possession of the box. It was supposed to hold the family's history. He had told her to keep it safe for him.

Frank peeled back the tissue paper covering the contents. Looked like some old albums. He picked up the first one and opened the cracked leather cover.

"Holy Mother of…"

There was the face. The one that had been haunting him. There was Sarah Haskins, lying in a field of flowers. There was Sarah Haskins, lying on a fur in front of a blazing fire. And there was Sarah Haskins, reading to a small boy. The drawings were beautifully done. The artist was obviously talented, and in love.

And then his eyes focused on the date. Each drawing had a date in the lower corner. Eighteen ninety. Eighteen ninety? What in the name of heavens were drawings of Sarah Haskins, from eighteen ninety, doing in his attic? Frank replaced the album, picked up the whole box, and took it down to his office.

****

She was cold. So cold. She coughed and began to strangle. Suddenly she was on her hands and knees, puking water all over the place. When she couldn't dredge up any more, she rolled to her side and collapsed back onto the floor. She lay there with her eyes closed, trying to get past the nausea and the feeling of panic.

Jeremy. Oh, Lord, where was he? She tried to sit up, but the whole room began to spin, so she closed her eyes again— Wait! Her eyes flew back open, then began to fill with tears.

"No!" She moaned it over and over as she curled into a fetal position. She'd seen enough to know she was home, but this place was no longer her home.

Sarah immediately grabbed her throat. Oh, Lord, it was gone. Then she remembered a small hand clutching at her, trying to help her out of the water.

Jeremy. Jeremy had her arrowhead. She began to sob, and after a while she fell into an exhausted sleep.

When Sarah woke again, it was to a coughing fit. She managed to sit up and look around her. She was in her kitchen, and she was covered in goosebumps. Her mind was slow to function.

It was so cold. Oh, no wonder, she thought. It's December. She had left in August. No one had been there to turn on the heat. Thank the Lord for the electric co-op; at least her electricity had not been turned off.

Sarah managed to stand and walk her way to the thermostat on the kitchen wall. It was hand over hand, by chair backs and countertops. She couldn't remember when she'd been so weak.

She raised the setting on the thermostat and listened. The furnace finally kicked in. Ahh, there was that first blast of stale air. Stale because she had not been here to change out filters and clean ducts. Because she had been with Aaron. Because she had found a better life. And she had lost it. She hadn't even acknowledged it, let alone accepted it, as what she had always wanted. And now it was gone.

Sarah staggered into her bathroom and started to fill the tub. As she undressed, she became aware of the silt and mud still clinging to her body. Please, Lord, she prayed. Please let Aaron and Jeremy be all right. Let them have survived the raging waters.

The house was finally beginning to feel warm by the time Sarah had scrubbed herself pink. She wrapped herself in a huge bath towel, then crawled under the bedcovers and let her mind take over. She was too tired to fight the painful memories. Somewhere in the middle of the revolving vignettes of Aaron looking at her tenderly or Jeremy bringing her little gifts of nature he had found, she drifted away to a soothing emptiness and slept.

****

Frank Kramer set the box on the floor in front of his desk. His mind was running a hundred miles an hour as he sat and looked at the box. He remembered the first time he'd seen the box. It had been during his last year at college. He'd been home for the summer, and his mother had not been feeling well.

"Frank, there is a box in the attic that belongs to you. If anything should happen to me, you must be careful not to let that box get misplaced or thrown out."

Of course, she hadn't bothered to tell Frank she'd already been diagnosed with cancer and would probably not make it past Christmas of that year.

"There are things in the box from your father's family, things that I'm sure you will want to see someday."

Frank vaguely remembered seeing the box when he placed all his things in storage after her death. He'd later moved everything into the basement of his and

Lisa's first home, but he was definitely going to take the time to go through the box now.

Lisa Kramer leaned against the doorway, shaking her head. "Frank, I leave you in here for two hours, and you wreck the place."

Frank raised his head from the papers he was holding. He met his wife's stern look, then looked around the room. The large box now stood empty, and there were stacks of notebooks and other assorted memorabilia scattered over the desktop and any other flat surface he could find.

He chuckled softly. "Sweetie, I'm sorry about the mess, but you won't believe the things I've found. A journal belonging to someone—a cousin, I'd guess—from over a hundred years ago. And look at this necklace."

Frank reached across the desk and picked up a rawhide strip. Dangling from the strip was a beautiful arrowhead. It was shot through with reds and yellows.

Lisa walked over and took it from his hand. "Now, that is truly a find, I agree." She smiled down at him as she placed the cord over his head, then positioned the carved rock against his chest. "Hmm…makes you look very rugged, and just a little sexy," she breathed thickly. She bent to kiss him slowly and thoroughly.

Frank tried to pull her onto his lap, but she grabbed both his hands and shoved them away. "Oh, no, buddy. It's your turn to cook supper, and you're not passing the buck today!"

It would be late into the night before he sat back down to read the journals. Before he would find that the woman in the drawings was named Sarah, and that she had told a strange story to Aaron Kramer.

****

When Sarah woke again, she was feverish, and her throat felt as if she had been swallowing concrete. It was all she could do to drag herself into the bathroom and check the medicine cabinet. Thank the Lord! Cough syrup, with some good old-fashioned drugs in it. She unscrewed the lid and took a big swallow, and as she did so, she remembered her first day with Aaron. He had made his own concoction for his painful throat.

Sarah braced herself with a hand on each side of the sink. She wanted to scream and wail. She wanted to curse the fates. She wanted to demand that she be taken back home. Back to Aaron and Jeremy.

She raised her head and looked at herself in the mirror. She had lost those fifteen or twenty pounds the doctor had fussed about. She had a better tan than she'd had in years. She was leaner and stronger than she'd been in high school. She also looked like a wild woman. There were circles under her eyes, and they were puffy from two days of endless tears. This had to stop or she would lose her mind.

Okay, coffee, she thought, as she pushed away from the sink. Coffee was a good place to start.

Sarah took her cup of coffee and walked into the den. There was the painting, still on the wall. It actually had meaning now. It was as if the stag stared at her over the Indian maiden's shoulder.

"What?" Sarah barked at the painting. "What the hell do you want from me? I know, they're alone now. Jeremy is probably catatonic, and Aaron has no idea how to handle it."

Sarah looked quickly around her, as if there would be anyone to hear her speaking to the painting. *Oh, good grief, I have to get out of here.* She could not contact anyone; there would be too many questions, with no believable answers. Just how was she supposed to explain walking away from a nine-year job and not returning?

She had seen the fingerprint powder on the doors and countertops. There had been an investigation started. What was she supposed to say? "I would have been back, but I got caught up in a hanging in eighteen ninety. Oh, and I killed two men while I was there." Yeah, sure. And then they would have her locked away. But sooner or later someone was going to know she was here, and she would have to say something.

Chapter Eleven

Aaron was wakened from a fitful sleep by a scream, the same scream he had been hearing each night for a week now.

"Sarah! Sarah," Jeremy screamed.

Aaron rolled over and pulled his son to his chest. "Wake up, son. It's just a dream. Wake up," he crooned as he rocked the boy in his arms. And, as had happened the past seven nights, Jeremy ended up soothing his pa.

"It'll be okay, Pa. She'll be back," the boy whispered in the dark hours just before dawn. "She'll find a way back, 'cause she loves us."

Aaron could not have measured his joy at hearing his son's voice for the first time in two long years, but he wanted to tell the boy to stop talking, just stop saying those things that he did not believe. He had the arrowhead. He had both of them, wrapped in a piece of linen and put away.

Sarah's story of how they were supposed to be worn by eternal lovers was just hogwash. He'd wanted to throw them both into Paint Creek when he saw hers clutched in Jeremy's little hand, but the boy would have lost his mind if Aaron had taken it from him that night.

The necklaces had no special powers. She was gone. If they were supposed to join lovers together, then why was she gone? The good Lord above knew how much he loved Sarah, and he would have sworn she felt the same way. She was gone now, and he could never tell her. And he would not allow himself to hope.

He tucked the blankets in around Jeremy again. The boy had already gone back to sleep. If not for him, Aaron would have been tempted to take his own life. He knew he couldn't leave the boy alone at such a young age. No, he would wait. Wait until the boy was able to care for himself. Then...then Aaron would ease his own suffering.

****

There was nothing else for it, she was gonna have to go to the store. She'd wait until dark, then drive over the mountain to Asheville. She wasn't apt to run into anyone who would recognize her, and she needed groceries. She'd taken everything out of the fridge three days ago, driven to the back ten acres, and buried it all. She had one can of soup left, and it did not appeal to her at all.

She'd have to drive very carefully, because they'd taken her driver's license. She'd found her purse on the dining room table, with all the contents poured out. The license had been removed from her wallet, and her computer was missing, which was not uncommon in an investigation of a missing person. Oh, dear Lord, how did she get caught up in such a convoluted series of actions? Well, she knew the how; it was the why that she couldn't get a handle on. Why take her there, let her fall in love, then jerk her back to a reality she did not want to face?

She'd never enjoyed buying groceries, but this trip was the worst. She found herself picking things up and thinking, *Jeremy would love this,* or, *Aaron would laugh if he saw this excuse for biscuits, in a can.* By the time she was loading the truck, she'd started crying again.

Dammit, she had to get a grip. Yes, her heart was broken, but this was not like her, to wallow in self-pity for days at a time. She turned the key, then sat a minute to let the engine warm up. All at once, it occurred to her—she could go back to the antique store. She'd make that woman tell her what to do. Sarah blew her nose, wiped her eyes, and headed across town. She drove straight to the little brick-lined alley. No store. Sarah drove down the alley, which ended abruptly at the back wall of another business. No windows or doors. No little sign reading "Anna's Gifts and Notions." No Indian woman to tell her how to fix this pain in her heart.

She turned her truck toward home. Just at the edge of Asheville, she saw the flashing light at what used to be her favorite little hamburger joint. Sarah laughed bitterly. She may as well splurge and have her favorite meal. At the drive-thru window, she ordered a double all the way, fries, and a chocolate shake. It would be some comfort during the long drive home.

Sarah had just placed the last bag of groceries on the counter when nausea hit her and she barely made it to the bathroom in time to lose the food she had so enjoyed on the trip home. She held back her long hair as she heaved again and again. Lord, she couldn't remember ever being this sick to her stomach, but then, she hadn't had that much greasy food in several months. It had been good going down, but it was definitely not so great on the way back up.

She washed her face, brushed her teeth, and headed to the kitchen to put away the groceries.

Sarah looked at the clock beside her bed. It was almost midnight as she turned out the light and, once again, cried herself to sleep.

When she opened her eyes again, the sun was shining through the open curtains, and it appeared to be a beautiful day outside. Sarah swung her legs over the side of the bed and slid her feet into her slippers. She made it to a full stand before the nausea hit her. She held on to the dresser to steady herself and took several deep breaths, trying to convince herself it would pass. It seemed to be working until, all at once, bile hit the back of her throat.

She just made it to the toilet. There was nothing to come up but the water she'd had after being sick last night. Just pure bile and water. She was exhausted by the time she'd spent five minutes dry heaving. Again she washed her face and brushed her teeth. She leaned with both hands on the sink, staring at her pale face in the mirror. What in the world was that all about? The greasy food had left her last night. There was no cramping, so it wasn't food poisoning, just instant nausea upon waking. She shook her head and headed back to the bedroom.

Sarah laid out some jeans and a T-shirt and was in the process of easing the shirt over her head when her hand slipped and her arm slammed into her right breast.

"Ouch." Sara finished putting on the shirt. She started to rub her still aching breast. "Ouch," she yelled again. What the heck? She was so sore. She didn't usually get sore with her period. Her period... No. NO. She could not be pregnant! Life would not do that to her.

Sarah climbed back into bed and cried herself to

sleep. Again.

****

Frank Kramer was sitting at his desk, lost in thought. He'd been through the contents of the box several times during the last week. He'd read the journals, and he felt like a voyeur as he leafed through the pages of drawings. Those of the woman, whoever she was, were evocative, filled with the love the artist had for his subject. And that subject looked like a reverse reincarnation of Sarah Haskins.

It was the journal entries that had held his attention, though. They were coherent, and easily understood, right up until the infamous flood, on December seventeenth, eighteen ninety. The entries were spotty after that, which was, in itself, understandable. Frank had checked with the local historical society and found that over one hundred folks had been killed in that disaster. From the last dated entries, it would seem that the Sarah Haskins double had been lost, just disappeared with the flood, her body never found. Kind of like Sarah had disappeared here.

The phone rang. Frank had been so deep in thought that the ringing startled him. He jumped in his chair, bumped his knee on the desk, and almost spilled his coffee. He shook his head as he grabbed for the still-ringing phone. He hoped something would break on the missing person case soon. This woman was starting to haunt his daydreams, as well as his nights.

****

Sarah nibbled on a cracker, hoping she would be able to keep it down. She had to know for sure. After all, she had nearly drowned, and undoubtedly swallowed a lot of nasty water. And then she had made a pig of herself with that heavy meal.

She was going to have to go back to Asheville and get a pregnancy test kit. Having made up her mind, she stretched out in the recliner to wait for nightfall.

Sarah checked her wallet. Twenty-seven dollars in cash left after the groceries. Well, that should certainly be enough to buy what she needed.

The long drive to Asheville gave her plenty of time to think. What in the world was she going to do? She had a good bit of money in the bank, but that wouldn't last forever. She wasn't sure Sheriff Lassiter would take her back again, especially when she had no explanation for her disappearance. And she didn't. At least none she wanted to share. And dispatching was all she'd ever done. Maybe it was time…

A large doe vaulted into the road and froze in the middle of the highway. Sarah slammed on her brakes, then immediately released them and swerved into the outside lane, just missing the beautiful animal by inches. Thank the Lord there was no oncoming traffic.

As soon as the danger to both herself and the animal was past, she began to shake. She was clutching the steering wheel so hard she could barely edge into the next pull-out spot. She put the truck in Park, turned off the engine, laid her head on the steering wheel, and began to sob. After a couple of minutes, she began to laugh hysterically and shake her head. She could probably save the money for the test kit. She had to be pregnant. She had never cried so much in her whole life as she had the last several days. Her hormones must be off the charts.

An hour later, she was leaving a discount drugstore with test kit in hand. She was starving but a little afraid to eat anything. She had a good hour's drive home, and she didn't want to have to stop on top of the mountain to puke her guts out. Coming up to the last gas station before the mountain, she glanced at her gas gauge out of habit. *Shoot fire and save matches!* She was dead on empty. She wheeled in and, without thought, yanked out a credit card and filled the truck.

By the time she drove into the yard, she was practically falling asleep at the wheel. The test could just wait until tomorrow. All she needed now was to rest her poor, tired body.

****

Frank Kramer answered the ringing phone.

"This is Agent Kramer," he said, in his best "I'm very busy, get to the point" voice.

"Agent Kramer, this is Arthur Porter, head of security at the Johnson Savings and Trust. Several weeks ago, you asked us to monitor a specific account for any activity. Do you recall that, sir?"

"I certainly do, Mr. Porter."

"Well, sir, someone used a credit card attached to that account to buy gas in Asheville. That was at approximately eleven-thirty last evening."

Frank was on his feet before Mr. Porter had finished his sentence. He grabbed the Haskins file and flipped it open.

His heart began to race, and even he could hear the tremor in his voice.

"Please read the account number to me, just to confirm that we are speaking of the same account."

"Oh, I assure you…"

Frank snapped, "The number, please."

There was a pause. Apparently, Mr. Porter was not

used to people snapping at him, but after his momentary hesitation he gave the number.

"Thank you, Mr. Porter. I will be stopping by later today to pick up a copy of that transaction. And thank you again for your prompt notification."

Frank sat back in his chair. A grin slowly crept across his face. Hot damn. This could be it. Okay, first things first. Pick up the paperwork from the bank. See if the gas station has video. Yes, sir, this must mean it's gonna be a great day.

Frank grabbed his overcoat, locked his office door, and headed to his SUV. Anyone watching might have remarked on the spring in his step.

****

Sarah looked for the third time at the test strip in her hand. She had no more tears. She had moved into numb territory.

Why me? She'd asked herself that several times in the last few days. *I've lived a relatively good life, never gone out of my way to hurt anyone, and wouldn't wish this on my worst enemy. If I even had an enemy. So why, Lord? After all the years alone, why would you put me in a place to fall in love with a man, then snatch me back to a loveless life?*

All good questions, but there would be no forthcoming answers. Sarah stood and dropped the stick into the bathroom trash. Looking at it wasn't going to fix anything. She was going to have a baby, and that was that.

Having accepted that thought, Sarah moved to the kitchen. She had to start eating better. She hadn't eaten enough in the past two weeks to nurture herself, let alone a baby. And she needed some vitamins or something, didn't she?

As she peeled vegetables for a pot of homemade soup, Sarah's mind began to wander. What would Jeremy and Aaron be eating tonight? Had Jeremy really gotten his voice back, or had she just imagined him screaming her name? Had Granny survived the flood?

If someone had asked, she would have sworn it was the onions that started the tears to fall again.

****

"I am Agent Frank Kramer, with the FBI." Frank held his badge out for the clerk to examine. "I need to see your video footage from last night."

The young woman didn't seem overly impressed.

"The manager is in the back office. If you want to see anything, you'll have to speak to him." She immediately turned to the customer waiting patiently behind Frank.

Frank nodded, then headed down the hallway to the office.

The manager didn't look a day over twenty and was busy eating a pizza. He looked surprised when Frank stopped in his doorway.

"Hey, you can't be back here."

Frank hauled out the badge again, flipped open the holder, and held it near the young man's face for several seconds.

"Oh," the young man said, around a mouthful of pizza. He grabbed a paper towel from a roll on the desk and wiped his hands and mouth before sitting back and staring at Frank.

Frank was too excited to mess with the kid's mind, so he got straight to the point.

"I need to see your security video footage from last

night, say about eight until midnight."

"Oh," the young man said again. "Is there some sort of problem?"

"Not if you have the video." Frank relented. "You're okay, kid. I just need to see who used a credit card at your pumps last night."

Frank could see the kid's face relax.

"Well, I just changed the video out before I started lunch, so that's easy enough."

Frank watched as the kid picked up a DVD from the cluttered desktop and placed it in the machine on the shelf behind the desk.

The small television to the right flickered, then began to show vehicles filling up at the three pumps in front of the store.

The kid turned to Frank and asked, "What time did you say?"

"Fast forward to eleven twenty-five last night, then just let it run."

Frank sat back in the chair, took out a notebook, and waited patiently.

The kid had no idea what they were looking for, so when Frank jumped to attention at eleven twenty-nine, it startled the poor boy into spilling his drink over the remainder of his pizza, not to mention the receipts scattered all over the desktop. He jumped up, flailing, trying to rescue some of the paperwork.

"Freeze!" Frank yelled, kind of like you would expect an agent to yell just before he shot you, and the kid must have believed he was not long for this world, because he froze with arms in midair and a look of pure terror on his ashen face.

"Just give me the remote, and you can leave."

This seemed to frighten the kid even more. "I…I'm not supposed to leave anyone unattended in here," he choked out.

"Oh, for the love of… Okay, give me the remote. Now mop that mess up and sit down. And be still."

Two minutes later, the kid plopped down in his chair with the kind of expression you would expect to find on a six-year-old placed in time out.

Frank looked at him sternly. "Okay, are you done now?"

The kid just nodded.

Frank backed up the DVD to twenty-three hours and twenty-seven minutes, then pressed Start. And at twenty-three hours and twenty-nine minutes, he jumped from his chair with a startled, "Damn!"

There on the small screen was a red-and-white 1985 Ford F-150 with four-wheel drive. Frank had seen that truck before. He knew just where he'd seen it last. Parked behind Sarah Haskins' cabin.

Then came the real shocker. The driver got out of the truck, walked to the pumps, and turned toward the camera as she opened the gas cap. At first the face was shielded from the cameras by a fall of long dark hair, but the person raised her face to look around as the tank filled.

"Damn!" Frank shouted again.

The kid kept looking from Frank to the TV screen and back again. She didn't look real dangerous to him, but the agent sure was excited.

Frank stopped the player and removed the DVD. He quickly scribbled something onto a sheet of his notebook, ripped it out of the book, and handed it to the kid.

"Here, bud. This is a receipt for the DVD."

The kid didn't even look at it. "Wait a minute, what if we need that?"

"Then you'll know where to find it, won't you?" Frank grinned.

The kid didn't even think about arguing. Heck, no skin off his nose. He had a receipt from the F-B-freakin'-I, in case his boss gave him a hard time. He watched Frank climb into a black SUV and burn rubber as he squealed onto Interstate 40 and headed west.

Chapter Twelve

Viking Valley, December 1890

"Pa," Jeremy called, for the third time.

Aaron finally turned his face toward his son.

Jeremy wished he could find the right words to ease his pa's pain. The firelight shining on his face showed up all the lines that seemed to have appeared overnight. Pa looked tired and old.

"Do we need to go hunting in the morning? We've got plenty in the root cellar, but we need some fresh meat."

Aaron returned Jeremy's gaze. Here was his son, who had not spoken a word in two years, and now the poor kid had to practically beg his pa to talk to him.

Man, you are an ungrateful bastard. Lord, forgive me for being a fool.

He laid the sketchpad face down on the table and walked over to sit on the bench by the hearth.

"I'm sorry, son. Sorry that I haven't been much company for you lately. Yes, I reckon we had better go find us some meat in the morning. Christmas is only a couple of days away, and a big turkey or a duck would be nice. We'll stop by Granny's on the way home and let her know that we'll provide the bird if she'll do all the fixin's."

Jeremy grinned. "She'll like that, Pa."

"All right, then, boy. I'll bank the fire. Then let's get some shuteye."

****

Aaron kept an eye on both sides of the trail as he followed along behind his son. He never let the boy get much out of eyesight now. The two days he'd spent searching for Jeremy and Sarah had been the worst in his life. He'd heard that Taggart's body had been found after the flood, but since he hadn't actually seen it, he was taking no chances.

He changed the two ducks he was carrying from his left shoulder to his right. Between the two, they must weigh fifteen pounds. Must mean a hard winter was coming. Those ducks had been fattening up for the long haul. He'd have to gather up some of the trees downed by the flood and start stacking more wood for the fires. He'd use Granny's old mule to help drag up the trees...

Jeremy had stopped walking and stood frozen in place.

Aaron immediately scanned the sides of the trail but saw nothing. He watched as Jeremy turned his face to the north, and there it was—on a rise, maybe forty yards away, stood the stag.

Aaron saw Jeremy step off the trail and start moving up the rise.

"Son," he spoke softly.

The boy stopped, then turned toward his pa. "It's okay, Pa. I won't be long."

Aaron felt totally useless as his son moved away. He did not understand the hold the stag had on the boy, and he wasn't sure he'd believe any explanation the boy might give, so he just never asked. He hung the ducks on a low tree branch, squatted with his back against the tree, and waited.

****

Greeneville, Tennessee, December 2016

The house smelled good, anyway, Sarah thought. The soup was keeping warm on the back burner, and there was a chocolate cake in the oven. The cake had been an afterthought. It had always been her favorite, but there had been a few moments when her stomach roiled at the smell as she first opened the can of powdered cocoa. It had settled down, but now she had no appetite. Not to mention she was tired. This was crazy. She'd never had an energy problem in her life. And now the least little exertion wore her out. Well, the good thing about being "missing" to the world, was that you didn't have to account to anyone. As soon as the cake was done, she would just go take a nap.

****

Frank called the sheriff's office and asked for the communications supervisor.

"This is Sergeant Thomas."

"This is FBI Agent Frank Kramer. I will be out at 31145 Harlan Road, reference a security check. Can you monitor a secondary channel?"

"Yes, sir. Go to channel six, and I'll have that monitored. Do you need backup?"

"10-54, no assistance necessary at this time. I'll advise you when to clear the channel."

He had kicked over all the what-ifs in his mind. He was pretty darn sure the girl was alone. If she'd been held prisoner or some such, she wouldn't have been gassing up the truck alone. Nevertheless, he stopped the SUV when he turned off the main road, put on his vest, and checked his nine-millimeter.

When he turned the last bend and had a visual on the house, he eased the vehicle off the dirt lane, secured it, and continued on foot. He swung wide through the elaborate garden area, making a mental note that the gardens had obviously not had attention in a long time.

As he approached from the rear, he noted that the truck had been moved since he was last here. He stopped about ten feet from the back door. He listened intently for several seconds. No noise. He drew his weapon and approached the door.

He stepped quietly up to the door, the aroma of chocolate wafting past him. Still no sound. He turned the knob, and the door opened. He gently closed the door, stepped to the side, and banged on the door sharply.

"Hello, inside the house! This is FBI Agent Frank Kramer. Please step to the door."

****

Viking Valley, Tennessee, December 1890

His heart told him the stag would not hurt Jeremy, but it still made him nervous as the boy got closer. When he was about five yards away, the huge animal folded his front legs and rested on the ground. Jeremy paused, then sat beside the animal, laying his head against that massive chest. The two of them just stared into each other's eyes for several long minutes while the boy rubbed the animal's neck and head.

Jeremy finally stood and stepped back, while the animal gracefully raised itself from the ground. After a few seconds, Jeremy turned to walk back to his father.

Aaron kept his eye on the stag. The animal stared at Jeremy's retreating back for a few moments before it turned and faded back into the forest.

When Jeremy was close enough, Aaron could see his young face was wreathed in a smile.

The boy walked straight to Aaron and placed both arms around his father's neck, and Aaron pulled him in for a long hug. As he held the boy tightly, he heard him whisper, "It's gonna be all right, Pa. She's coming home."

Aaron's whole frame tensed. He took Jeremy by the shoulders and held him at arm's length.

"What did you say?" Aaron could hear the harsh sound of his own voice.

Jeremy smiled at his pa. "The a-ha-wi told me that Sarah is coming home soon, and that you ought not worry."

Aaron started to ask what the boy meant by "told," then figured he didn't really want to know. The boy was obviously his mother's son, and who was he to question what seemed perfectly logical to the child. However, the stag had not told him a damn thing, and he was not going to get his hopes up.

****

Greenville, Tennessee, December 2016

Sarah was snatched from a deep sleep by…what? She was wild-eyed, searching the room. Was that someone yelling? Good Lord, had she locked the back door?

She stood and picked up her pistol from the nightstand, all in one fluid motion. Fluid, but too quickly. The room spun just a little, and she had to close her eyes to stop the movement. Was that the loose floorboard in the mudroom squeaking? Her eyes flew open as she put her back to the wall and edged around the bedroom door and into the hall. She caught sight of a flash of movement in the big mirror hanging on the opposite wall. It was a man holding a gun, edging toward the hallway. He turned to look to his left, and Sarah caught his face, full on, in the mirror.

She was so startled she spoke aloud. "Aaron!"

She saw the man freeze.

"Who's there? Put your hands up and step out where I can see you."

Before she could think of a response, their eyes met in the mirror.

Now that they were looking directly at each other, she could see that it wasn't Aaron, but the resemblance caused her eyes to fill with tears. She was still frozen to the spot when the man spoke again.

"Sarah Haskins, I am FBI Agent Frank Kramer. Put down the weapon and walk slowly toward me," he ordered loudly. Then, "Is there anyone else in the house?"

Sarah's knees weakened as realization set in. She'd known they would come sooner or later, but she was not mentally prepared for the questions that would follow.

Sarah walked slowly to the table underneath the mirror and placed her pistol down gently. She kept her body turned so the agent could see her hands in the mirror.

"All right, I'm stepping out now." Sarah moved slowly out into the open floor and turned to face the man.

He was still holding the gun in front, standing sideways, in the perfect shooter's stance.

Sarah said, "I'm feeling a little woozy. May I sit

down, please?" She nodded in the direction of the dining room table.

"Sure," he replied. "Just move slow and keep your hands where I can see them."

Frank had already noted her pallor and shaking hands.

Sarah pulled out a chair and sat, keeping her hands above the table at all times. She watched as he moved to pick up her pistol, unload it, and place both the bullets and the gun in his pocket.

"Is there anyone else in the house I need to know about? You don't mind if I just do a quick check, right? I'll tell you how this is going to go," he said, as he stopped behind Sarah. "Put your hands behind your back. I'm gonna cuff you, and once I've checked the premises, I'll take them off, okay?"

Sarah just nodded. As if she had a choice, she thought.

He was back in under five minutes. He removed the cuffs, then walked to the opposite side of the table and sat down. He took a radio from his belt and spoke into it.

"This is Agent Kramer. S.O., do you read me?"

"Yes, sir, this is dispatch. Go ahead."

"Thanks for the coverage. You can clear the channel now."

"10-4, sir, clearing channel."

Sarah's stomach rolled over at this exchange. She recognized Beverly's voice. Lord, what must they have thought when she never showed up?

He took a small tape recorder from his pocket and turned it on.

"This is Agent Frank Kramer. This is Friday,

December twenty-third, thirteen hundred thirty-three hours. I am speaking with Sarah Haskins, in her home at three-one-one-four-five Harlan Road, Greeneville, Tennessee." He placed the tape recorder on the table between them.

"Well, Sarah—may I call you Sarah?" He didn't wait for an answer, just moved right on. "Some folks have been very worried about you. It seems you just fell off the face of the earth."

Under any other circumstances, Sarah would have recognized the humor in that. However, there was nothing humorous about this. She needed to keep focused and be careful what she said. Lying to the Federal Bureau of Investigation was a federal offense, even if you weren't under oath.

After a long, empty pause, he continued. "Sarah, can you tell me what happened, or where you've been?"

Sarah closed her eyes and inhaled and exhaled deeply. When she opened them, she looked at the man and thought, What the heck, I have nothing to lose here, I'll just tell him the truth.

"I started my vacation in August. The first day off, I drove to Asheville to hunt antiques. I found a little shop where a woman sold me a..." Sarah's voice faded. She closed her eyes again.

Frank watched her closely. Her hands were shaking worse, and while she seemed to be freezing, he was sweating heavily. It had to be eighty-five degrees in here.

Sarah was afraid to open her eyes. She had seen Anna standing behind the agent, shaking her head slowly from side to side.

Sarah forced herself to open her eyes. Thank the

Lord, the woman was gone. Good golly Moses, she must be losing her mind. She focused on the man again. She could see beads of sweat on his forehead.

"I'm sorry if you are uncomfortable. Feel free to take off your coat. I have been sick for the past few days and can't seem to get warm."

Frank Kramer stood, removed his coat, and hung it over a chair. He also took off the heavy vest and laid it on the table.

He sat back down. "You were saying you went shopping?"

"Yes, I did a little shopping, then returned home. I was going to go into town and eat but decided to just stay in and rest. I had been doing a lot of overtime and needed to catch up on my sleep. So I took out a bottle of Sangria, stretched out in the recliner, and slept." Sarah couldn't bring herself to go on.

"And then what, Sarah? What happened when you woke up?"

Sarah was beginning to get angry. What had happened wasn't her fault. It wasn't like anyone asked her if she'd like to take a little trip back through time. Or save a man from hanging. Or fall in love.

Frank observed her straightening herself a little in the chair. He could see the tightening of her jaw. Good. If she got pissed off, she might actually tell him something.

"Go ahead, Sarah. You got drunk, and then what happened?"

Her brows drew together sharply. "I did not get drunk! I'm not a drinker, I think I only had one glass. When I woke up, I was halfway up Viking Mountain, and a man was about to be hanged."

Frank Kramer had been an agent for too many years to let a suspect see him react, but she had sure hit a nerve with that line. He covered by reaching up and loosening his tie and unbuttoning his shirt collar.

He leaned forward in his chair. "How did you get up the mountain, Sarah? Are you saying you were kidnapped?"

Sarah opened her mouth to speak, then closed it again. Her eyes were locked on a rawhide cord, with a dangling arrowhead, hanging around Frank Kramer's neck. She wiped a hand across her eyes. No, it couldn't be, she told herself. How could he have her necklace? Her heart raced, and her brain moved even faster. What difference did it make how he got it? She had to have it. That was her ticket back. It had to be. Why else would this man be here with her necklace?

She took another steadying breath. "Remember I said I was shopping? Well, I found a necklace that I liked. It looked very much like the one you have on. Could I see that one, please?"

Frank had become so used to the arrowhead on its leather thong that it took a moment for him to process what she meant. He raised one hand to his chest. He began to get that feeling inside. The one that always led to something. He raised the rawhide cord over his head and slid the necklace across the table to Sarah. If it opened a line of communication between them, that would be great.

He noted that her hands were still shaking. He wondered if he should call emergency services to check her out. Her pupils were not dilated, so he didn't think she was on anything, but she looked haggard. Almost as if she were recovering from a long illness.

141

"This looks almost identical to the one I bought in Asheville. Is that where you got this one?"

"No. Actually, I think it belonged to an ancestor of mine. A cousin or great-great-uncle or something. I found it in a box of family things my mother left me when she passed on."

Frank noted a hint of a smile as the girl rubbed the arrowhead between her hands.

Holding the necklace, Sarah could feel this time what she did not before. Energy was pouring from the stone and into her—to be specific, into her stomach.

Sarah jumped up so quickly she knocked over her chair. She clamped a hand over her mouth as she started gagging. The other hand slipped the necklace into her pocket.

"Sick," she mumbled around her hand.

Frank Kramer was on his feet with the gun in his hand. He hoped he wasn't going to have to shoot this girl, the girl who had filled so much of his time and thoughts these last few months.

She saw the gun and raised wide, frightened eyes to his face. "I'm going to vomit," she explained weakly as she turned to make a run for the bathroom.

Frank was right behind her but was not quick enough to grab the door before the lock clicked. He could hear the sounds of painful retching and water splashing as she emptied her stomach, presumably into the toilet.

"Sarah, open the door!" he yelled as he beat on the door.

The only response he got was the continued sound of a person being violently ill. When the retching finally stopped, Sarah placed the necklace in the dirty clothes hamper.

"Sarah, open the door."

The door opened slowly, and Frank was hit with the sour smell that can only be associated with vomit. Sarah had turned back to the sink. She splashed water on her face, rinsed her mouth, and picked up her toothbrush.

"I'm sorry, but I told you I've been sick."

She proceeded to brush her teeth, while the agent stood in the doorway. When she was finished, she turned to him.

"Am I under arrest?"

Frank was actually sorry for her. She looked like warmed-over death.

"I don't believe I said anything about arresting you. However, I would like to continue our conversation. Maybe hear a little bit more about the hanging."

"Look, Agent Kramer, I'm sick. I need to get some rest. Could we do this tomorrow? I'll sit down with you and tell you everything you want to know, but tomorrow, please."

"Do I need to call someone to check you out? Maybe take you to the emergency room?"

"That's very kind of you, but not necessary. I think I ate something bad the other night, while I was in Asheville. I may have a slight case of food poisoning. I just need to drink plenty of liquids and get some rest."

Frank followed her back into the kitchen. He saw the truck keys hanging from a hook by the door.

Sarah watched him walk over and take the keys off the hook.

"All right, Sarah. I'll be back first thing in the morning to continue this conversation."

Frank collected his tape recorder, vest, and jacket, then turned to Sarah.

"I'm going to take your pistol, as well, just until the morning."

Sarah started to protest, then caught herself. If losing the pistol would get him out of here, so be it.

"Fine. I have a shotgun in the closet, in case someone tries to break in before you get here."

She immediately regretted the sarcasm, when she saw the look on his face.

"Just a figure of speech. I'm not expecting any company, good or bad," she hurried to assure him.

"Well, I'll tell you what. Since so many folks have been so worried about you, I'll just arrange to have a deputy sit at the end of your drive until I get here in the morning."

"That will be fine, and thank you for your concern." She smiled weakly. As long as the deputy stayed away from the house, it was fine with her.

Sarah made herself a cup of chamomile tea and sat at the breakfast table. There were things she had to do before she put on the necklace. She had no idea how this was supposed to work, or even if it would, but she had to try.

She took a long soak in a hot tub and gave her hair a hot oil treatment. She sat on the bed afterwards and eyed every item in her closet. It was winter. Her lifestyle would be completely different, and she had to prepare accordingly.

And then she remembered. Oh, good grief, whatever she wore would be useless in a few more weeks. All right, then take that into consideration, wear something loose as well as warm.

She never thought she'd be glad that she had not cleaned out Uncle Frank's closet. She found two oversized sweatshirts. Yes, these would be loose for a good while. She placed them on her bed. She took a long denim skirt out of the back of her closet. She had never been a walking fashion plate, but even she knew it was out of style today. She smiled to herself. It might not be stylish, but it would come in handy around the cabin.

Her eyes filled with tears. Just thinking she might make it back to Aaron and Jeremy had lifted her spirits. Lord willing, she would make it.

At seven that evening, she was dressed in two sweatshirts, a long denim skirt, and a pair of comfortable hiking boots. With another cup of tea in one hand and her necklace in the other, she sat back in the recliner and stared at the painting.

"Anna, if you can hear me, please know that I am ready to accept the gift you gave me. I did not realize how precious it was until I lost it. Be assured, that if I make it back, the rest of my life will be dedicated to filling their lives with love and joy."

Sarah placed the rawhide cord around her neck, finished her tea, and closed her eyes to wait for sleep.

Chapter Thirteen

Frank Kramer sipped his coffee as he drove. He hadn't slept well, and that was unusual for him. He'd stayed holed up in his office for hours last night, going over this case a dozen times.

The girl had broken no laws, and all anyone really wanted was to be sure she was okay. He couldn't say just how okay she was, as her behavior had been less than normal. Maybe she did have a mild case of food poisoning. Maybe losing the last of her family had nudged her over the edge, and she'd just taken a hike to get her head straight. As soon as she gave him some answers this morning, he would wind up his report and pass it on Sheriff Lassiter.

Frank eased his SUV alongside the deputy's vehicle and lowered his window. It was chilly this morning, and his breath left wisps of cloud as he spoke to the young man.

"Everything okay here?"

"Yes, sir, nothing in or out in the last twelve hours."

"Good. Go get yourself a hot breakfast and some shuteye, and thanks for the assistance."

Frank lined up some specific questions in his mind as he drove the half mile to the house. At the top of that list was a reminder to get his necklace back from the girl. He'd forgotten all about it until he stepped into the shower last night. He wanted to pass it on to his boy someday.

Frank drove up to the back door this time. No need to surprise her. He knocked on the back door, then waited. And waited. He knocked again, louder.

"Sarah, it's Frank Kramer. Open up."

Frank removed his weapon from its holster, then tried the doorknob. It turned, and he eased the door open slowly. Maybe she was a sound sleeper, but Frank didn't think that was the problem. His first clue was the temperature. The house was cold, as if it had been abandoned. He made note of a cake carrier on the counter and an envelope lying on top of it, but he continued through to the hallway.

"Sarah," he called as he moved on slowly, in that perfect shooter's stance.

When he got to her bedroom, he found the door open, the bed neatly made, and no Sarah.

Damn! In the den, he found an empty teacup on the side table, and an extended recliner with no one in it. He cleared the rest of the house, then moved back to the kitchen.

He stood in front of the cake carrier for several long moments. The envelope was labeled with one word: Frank. He put his weapon back in its holster and picked up the envelope. He cursed his own stupidity as he opened it.

****

Viking Valley, Christmas Eve, 1890

It was the barking that dragged Sarah from sleep. As her mind floated toward consciousness, the cold began to seep into her bones. Cold. Barking.

Sarah awoke with a jerk and was immediately glad

she had wrapped two scarves around her neck last night. She sat up to look around. She expected to see some familiar location on the trail up Viking Mountain. What she saw reduced her to tears. She was about fifty yards from Granny's cabin, and Red was telling the world she was there.

"Red," Granny shouted, "shut up, boy. You're scarin' the chickens."

And there was the dear old woman exiting the barn, carrying the egg basket. Sarah raised herself from the dried corn stubble. Her legs were stiff with cold, and she staggered a little.

Granny caught sight of the movement out in the field and raised a hand to shade her eyes from the rising sun.

"Who's out there?"

"It's me, Granny. It's Sarah." Sarah started moving toward the old woman.

Granny's grin lit up her whole face. "Well, child, it's about darn time you found your way home. Come on, git yourself out of the cold, and you can tell old Granny all about your adventures."

Sarah's laugh bordered on hysterical. The old woman seemed to think it had been a foregone conclusion that Sarah would return. She wished she had been so sure. It would have saved her days of sick grieving over what she feared had been lost forever. Well, she was here now, and that was what counted. She was ready to let go of that other world.

"Granny, I need to get to Aaron…"

"You don't need to go anywhere, child. The boys will be here in a couple of hours. They carried over two big, fat ducks yesterday. They're comin' for dinner, and boy-howdy, am I gonna have a treat for them. So come on in here and get yourself warmed up. You can keep old Granny company whilst she finishes dinner."

Granny put the eggs in the pantry and turned to see Sarah peeling off clothes.

"Well, you sure was preparin' for the snow that's comin'."

Sarah gave a weak smile. "I wasn't sure what I was preparing for, Granny. I was afraid to hope that I could make it back."

"Yes, Aaron was afraid to hope, as well. Jeremy kept tellin' his pa it would be okay." Granny saw the look of surprise on Sarah's face.

"Yep. The boy has been a-chatterin' up a storm since you been gone. It was the one blessin' out of the whole flood. Don't know yet how many folks got washed away, but I did hear tell they found the bodies of two of Taggart's men down in the bottomland. 'Course, don't think too many folks'll be grievin' for them. That pair was always lookin' for trouble. Looks like they done finally found it."

Granny looked up from the potato she was peeling. "Child, are you okay? You're lookin' a little green."

Before Granny had finished speaking, Sarah was running for the back door. She barely made it to the edge of the porch before the heaving started. When it was over, Sarah raised her head to find Granny standing there with a cup of water in her hand and a huge smile on her face.

"Well, it seems like we got more to celebrate than just Christmas."

Sarah took the cup of water and rinsed her mouth. "Granny, I'm not so sure how Aaron will take this news, so can you let me tell him, in my own time?"

"Why, sure, honey, but I can tell you right now that man will be beside himself with joy. Now, you come on back inside and brush that pretty hair. Then you just stretch out on the settee and rest, while I finish up dinner."

Sarah was in a light sleep state when a whoosh of cold air washed over her. She opened her eyes in time to see Jeremy skip across the floor and into the kitchen. He hadn't seen her on the settee, so she was able to watch him trying to steal a cookie from the table. Just the sight of that happy little face gave her joy.

Then the doorway filled with Aaron's wide shoulders. Her heart actually skipped a beat as her breathing quickened. She slowly lowered her feet to the floor and raised herself to a sitting position.

As Aaron turned to close the door behind himself, his attention caught on her movement. He turned his head toward her, and a shock of recognition washed over his face. He froze for about three seconds before he lunged for her and wrapped her in a bear hug, praying into her hair. "Thank you, Lord. Thank you, Lord."

He finally put her at arm's length and took complete inventory. "Are you okay? You weren't hurt? You're too pale. Have you been sick? Lord, how I've missed you."

Sarah tried not to sob as she continually wiped tears. "Can you just hold me, please?"

Aaron pulled her back into the circle of his arms. "Honey, I plan on holding you for the rest of our lives."

Aaron looked over Sarah's head, and there was Jeremy, grinning like he was the happiest little boy on the face of the earth. He held out a hand to his son, and the boy came running to throw his arms around both of them.

Granny smiled from the kitchen. She knew that time held no power over love.

Sarah would take her knowledge from the future and blend it with the love from the past, because she had a heart for all time.

****

Greeneville, Tennessee, December 24th, 2016

Frank Kramer sat in his home office and read the note one more time:

Dear Agent Kramer, please forgive me. It was not my intention to deceive you, but there was no other way. I noticed the wedding ring you were wearing. Please take the cake home with you. I will not be returning again. I will get your necklace back to you, in time. Sincerely, Sarah Haskins Kramer

What the hell was he supposed to make of that? How in the world could he explain, in a report, that he had let this girl disappear again?

"Excuse me."

Frank looked up at Lisa, standing in the doorway, a plate in each hand, a large wedge of chocolate cake on each plate.

"Frank Junior is now sound asleep, so I think we should spend some time together. I'm not going to say I'm real excited about you bringing home a cake that some runaway dispatcher made, but then it *is* chocolate."

Frank laughed. "Yes, so it is." He took his plate and fork in hand.

"Mmm, that is a darn good cake. So how about you

tell me everything about this woman who has been living in your head for months now."

Frank looked at his beautiful, pregnant wife. He was glad she was over the morning sickness. Frank froze, with a forkful of cake halfway to his mouth.

"Damn! That's what it was. She's pregnant."

Lisa tilted her head, arched an eyebrow, and said sternly, "Is there something you need to tell me, Franklin Kramer?"

Frank almost spit chocolate cake across the room. He laughed, as he wiped his mouth with a napkin. "No, you silly goose, I don't have any deep, dark confessions to make. You win—I'll tell you all about this girl."

When Frank had told her everything, she asked, "What does she look like?"

"Oh, I can show you, but you're not gonna believe this. You know that box my mom had marked for me? Well, I found these drawings in the box…drawings that look just like Sarah Haskins."

Frank picked up the box and carried it to the sofa, where he set it at Lisa's feet. Frank sat on the floor and opened the box. There was a yellowed paper package lying on top, tied with rawhide cord. And attached to the cord was a Tennessee Paint Rock arrowhead.

"Frank, isn't that your necklace you said you lost?"

Frank just stared at the necklace. "This was not here yesterday."

Lisa looked at Frank. He had visibly paled, and as he picked up the package, his hand actually trembled.

Frank carefully untied the cord and eased back the edges of the paper. He found a stack of drawings. A series of drawings of Sarah: Sarah as a glowing mother-to-be; an older Sarah playing checkers with a young man who could be the boy in the earlier drawings; then an older Sarah with a beautiful little girl, picking flowers. And each drawing was dated, in the lower right corner, with dates of 1890 onward, through at least fifteen years. The last drawing in the stack was a Sarah who had lived many years, possibly sixty, as it was dated 1940. There were smile lines around her mouth, and her eyes seemed to twinkle with happiness. Underneath that drawing was a handwritten page. One look told Frank Kramer that the handwriting was Sarah's. He began to read aloud.

Dear Frank, I could have told you that I travelled back to 1890 and saved an innocent man from hanging. But would you have believed me? And I could have told you that I fell in love, for the first time in my life, and that I would risk that life to get back to him. But would you have believed me? And that all this was achieved by the necklace you now hold in your hands.

Our lives will be forever entwined, Frank. First because an Indian spirit-woman chose your ancestor to father her child. Then, well, because you were a decent man. A man who gave a desperate, frightened woman the opportunity to love with her heart for all time.

I'll be forever in your debt,
Sarah Haskins Kramer

Frank looked at Lisa. There were trails of tears down her face. He took her hand in his and leaned back against the sofa.

"This is going to be one hell of a report," Frank said with a chuckle.

A word about the author...

Linda was born in Goody, Kentucky, in the heart of coal mining country. Her mother moved her to Cleveland, Ohio when she was a small child. In the summer she ran barefoot on her grandparents' farm and during the school year she attended concerts and visited museums. She was able to experience the best of both worlds.

Her careers have been just as varied. She spent eighteen years in the manufacturing end of the fashion industry, which fed her love of color and style. From there she went on to spend twenty years as a Crime Scene Investigator, which gave her an insider's perspective on the abuse of women and children.

You will find her stories are of strong women who have overcome adversity to find the love and stability they deserve, and there will often be a milliner involved.

http://lindatillisauthor.com